The sweet memory of a summer friendship that lasts a lifetime

Christine Pisera Naman

*To: Laura
With Love,
Christine*

Kirk House Publishers
Minneapolis, Minnesota

The Believers
by Christine Pisera Naman

Copyright © 2011 Christine Pisera Naman. All rights reserved.

No part of this book may be reproduced or transmitted in any form by any means, electronic, mechanical, recording, or otherwise, without the express permission of the publisher. For information or permission for reprints or excerpts, please contact the publisher.

This is a work of fiction. Names, characters, and incidents are either the product of the author's imagination or are used fictitiously, and any resemblance to anyone living or dead is entirely coincidental.

ISBN-13: 978-1-933794-35-8
ISBN-10: 1-933794-35-6

Library of Congress Control Number: 2010943138

Kirk House Publishers, PO Box 390759, Minneapolis, MN 55439
Manufactured in the United States of America

To my mother who believes in me endlessly.

*And to all of the young ones out there
who feel as if they don't quite fit in.
I promise you will grow in to the world
and the world will grow in to you.
And you will be amazing.*

Prologue

Each night I think of two things—where I am and where I came from. Where I am most nights is standing slightly offstage waiting for them to announce my name. In a few minutes, I will walk into the blaring spotlight and do what I love most—sing. I will sing my heart out to thousands of people. It is an honor. I have been blessed with a good voice, a gift from God. I am privileged that He has chosen to speak through me. To sing for others is simply a calling that I heard and answered.

When I think of where I came from, I smile because the same image always appears before me. It is the image of an awkward, shy boy—a boy who is small for his ten years of age, a boy who sometimes I barely remember knowing. It is the image of a boy whose mother would constantly smooth back his forever cow-licking hair and say, "Don't worry, you'll grow into the world little by little, and the world will grow into you, too." It is the image of a boy whose father loved him unconditionally but didn't understand him at all.

I remember a little boy who after school, instead of playing ball on the street or riding his bike to the park, would stand on his bed with his hair brush microphone and sing into his mirror and pretend to be Tony Bennett.

I may not remember every detail of that little boy, but I do know that his father grew to understand him and his mother was right because he did grow into the world and the world grew into him. And the boy grew into me.

Right before going on stage I always take a deep breath and say a humble prayer of thanks. I pray to do my best and to make my God proud. But I always pray to make someone else proud, too. I reach into the pocket of my trousers and rub my thumb and forefinger against a tiny faded photograph of a scrawny ten-year-old white boy sitting on the lap of a six-foot-seven black man who is taller and stockier than a tree. Both of them are grinning ear to ear in the photo taken from inside a camera booth in the lobby of a movie theater. It is a picture of me and my best friend—the only true best friend I ever had, the only best friend I will ever care to have, a best friend that no one even knew I had. It is a picture of me and Rupert Holmes III. I pray that I am making him proud because he is the reason I am standing there. He is my inspiration because one summer when I was ten years old, Rupert Holmes told me it was OK to be me and set the music free in me. So I am singing for him and God. Always. This is our story.

How It All Started

It was two weeks into summer vacation, a Sunday night. I was ten years old and I can remember exactly where I was standing in the kitchen of our home, next to the garbage can, throwing away a banana peel from a banana that I didn't deserve to be eating because my mother said I hadn't eaten enough of the dinner that she had made. But she gave it to me anyway. Looking back, I figure the reason that I can remember exactly where I was is because my heart had stopped beating, and I'm pretty sure I had stopped breathing as well. So I guess it would be natural to remember details of such an event.

"I have good news!" my mother announced cheerily to me. My father, brother, and sisters were in the kitchen, too, but she was talking only to me. "I called Edwin Jolson's mother today!" she said. Edwin was an older, smart-alecky boy who lived down the street with whom I got along by staying away from.

Now, in addition to not breathing and my heart having stopped, I was beginning to sweat.

"And I told her how I had noticed that Edwin walks by our house every morning on his way to the pool."

Now I was getting light-headed.

"And I asked her if she thought Edwin would mind if you went along, too, and she said she was sure that he wouldn't mind at all. She said she was sure that he would love having you go along with him and his friends. He's such a nice boy! They go to our church, you know. Well, of course, you know that."

Her words were coming out in a rush, and I could tell she was nervous and that she had actually planned this speech, but was trying to act casual as if we were just talking. The fact that I was paralyzed, motionless, and mute, and just staring at her through glassy marble eyes could not be helping to calm her nerves. But this was a nightmare of mine coming true right in the middle of my own kitchen.

"He seems like such a nice boy," she said again.

And inside I was screaming, "He is not. He is not a nice boy! He's a gigantic smart alec who knows how to act like a nice boy in front of grown-ups!" But none of that came out.

"Won't going to the pool every day with a group of boys be such a nice way to spend the summer?" she asked, too loudly to sound natural. "The summer of fifth grade was when I met my best friend, Marisol," she continued. I had heard that story a million times. My mother was dying for me to have a best friend. Not having a best friend was not a problem for me, especially now that it was summer, because I got to be upstairs in my bedroom with my music without the interference of school. But from where my mother was standing, which was obviously at the front window looking out at Edwin and his friends passing by our house heading happily to the pool to be best friends, this looked like a problem. I was smart enough to know that in my mom's eyes, Edwin Jolson did not look like an odd duck while I, her son, did. There were five kids in our family, and I guess you could say I was the odd one compared to the rest of my siblings. But I was a happy odd duck. I was a content and peaceful odd duck. But, compared to the rest of my siblings, I guess I stood out. My older sister was just a regular girl with normal activities and normal friends. My older brother was pretty much the same thing—a regular guy, a little athletic, with normal friends. And my little twin sisters were just two goofy little girly girls with gaggles of other goofy little girlfriends. So I was the different one. I had a few friends but not close ones that I would take home from school or to whose houses I would be invited. So I guess from where my mom stood, she saw four of her five children making friends, being popular, going over to other kid's houses after school—in essence, being "normal."

On the other hand, she saw me being a hermit up in my room alone doing Lord knows what. I got along fine at school with the other kids but was relieved as could be to retreat to the safe haven of my room after school and do what I loved to do. And what I loved to do was to lay on my bed and listen to my music, write lyrics in a tablet that I kept hidden under my mattress, and dream about the day that I would stand on a stage and sing to an audience. And it was there that I was happiest.

Probably just by the nature of her gender, my mother worried more about me than my father did. Mothers are fixers and want to make something right they see as wrong. Fathers seem to be more helpless observers. My father saw that I was different, but I think I confused him more than anything. Every once in awhile I would catch just the briefest snippet of a hushed conversation between my parents, with my mother saying something about them taking me somewhere or signing me up for some group or club where I might fit in. My father's response was usually something like, "Let him be. He'll find his own way. We all have to."

If I didn't know how much my mother loved me, all of this might have hurt my feelings more than the little bit that it did. But I didn't let it bother me too much because I was sure of her love, and I knew deep down that she was just trying to fix something that she thought looked like it needed fixing.

I stood frozen in the kitchen, feeling that preteen combination of embarrassment and anger. "I don't want to go to the pool with Edwin," I said, not quite through gritted teeth but close. My father raised his eyes just slightly above the newspaper that he was reading at the kitchen table as a warning to me to watch my tone.

"Why not?" my mother exclaimed. "It would be such a nice, healthy way to spend the summer."

I wanted to shout at her, "You mean it would be a 'normal' way to spend the summer, because you think me being alone in my room with my music is weird!" But of course I didn't say this, not only because I knew it would hurt her feelings, but also because my dad was still glaring over his paper at me. She just had no idea how much stress this was causing me. The thought of going to the pool with this kid was actually starting to make my stomach hurt.

"Because I don't want to go to the pool with Edwin," I answered. My dad, realizing that this was not going to end quickly and that it might be getting louder, motioned to my sister and brother to leave the room and to take my little sisters with them. I wondered if, when I was a dad, if I would be able to clear a room with just a look and to say all of that with just a nod. I had no idea whose side he was on, but at least he realized that we didn't need an audience.

"Why not?" my mother pressed. "He's such a nice boy."

I wanted to start yelling again, "No, he is not such a nice boy," but I knew that going there wasn't going to help. Edwin was the kid that was most opposite of me. We had nothing in common. But how could I ever explain to her that the very last way I wanted to spend my summer was hanging out at the pool with Edwin and that I could completely promise her that the last thing Edwin wanted in this whole world was to be saddled with me.

I tried a different approach.

"He is a nice kid," I agreed. "I just don't want to go to the pool with him. I don't want to go to the pool with anyone. I don't really like the pool."

But she, who could usually read me better than anyone in the entire world was blinded with trying to fix a part of my life that she was sure was broken. She had no idea that she was torturing me. "Look, she said excitedly, disappearing from the kitchen. She returned a moment later holding a cotton drawstring sack with a fish on it. She quickly undid the string and dumped the contents onto the kitchen table. A blue bathing suit with whales on it, a bottle of sunscreen, a pair of swim goggles, and a beach towel with a gigantic starfish spilled out. "I got all of this," she announced, turning the bag slightly inside of itself to reveal a zipper pocket. She unzipped it and pulled out some bills. "There's three dollars for a snack," she said happily, as if this would surely seal the deal.

She was killing me. I loved her so much and knew what she was trying to do, and I didn't want to break her heart. But, honestly, I knew that more than anything I did not want to go to the pool with Edwin Jolson.

"Mom, please," I said, whining now. "I just don't want to go to the pool."

"Couldn't you just try it?" She was practically begging.

"Mom, no!" I shot back.

"How about you try it for just one day?" she offered.

"Mom—" I began again, but was cut off.

"Noah." It was my dad's voice. "Try it for tomorrow."

This was said in the quiet, even tone that my father always used when it was not a suggestion but a command. I looked at him through eyes that were blurry with anger and frustration. I felt that he was selling me out. I pleaded with him through my eyes to see my side. But he didn't. I glared. Usually he didn't tolerate "looks" from his children, but he let this one go. I knew better than to push him any further, so I looked away first. I had lost and I knew it. I looked at my mother upset and disappointed. She knew my father's word was law and that tomorrow I would be going to the pool with Edwin Jolson. I stormed out of the kitchen.

Later that night my mother crept into my darkened room. I was in bed but not asleep yet. I hadn't gone downstairs to say goodnight as I usually did. I didn't move when she came in. She set the repacked pool bag on the floor by the door and crept over to the bed. She leaned over, pushed my hair back, and kissed me on the forehead.

"I just thought it would be nice to spend the summer having a best friend," she murmured softly. Then she walked out of the room and closed the door with one soft click.

Rupert Holmes III

The next morning, I stood in the doorway of our house as my mother tried to straighten the collar of my collarless T-shirt. I stared at her in complete disbelief, wondering how she could not see how unhappy this was making me.

"Mom, please," I began to beg. But, as if she didn't hear me, she just chattered on happily about how she met her very first best friend and how they knew that they were best friends instantly and how they shared secrets, favorite books, and slumber parties and dances. She went on and on, and I became more and more miserable. I felt bad for her, but I felt worse for me. I knew that there was no use in telling her that Edwin and I were not meant in any way to be best friends. We were two totally different kids who never in a million years would choose to go to the pool and hang out together. And honestly, the way that she was talking about it was creeping me out. She had no idea that the only reason this entire thing was happening was because the mother of the not cool kid asked the mother of the very cool kid to let him go along, and she had no idea how humiliating that was. I wondered if the mother of the un-cool kid was always the last to know. Maybe one day the world would stop spinning for a second and decide to spin the other way and I would be the cool kid and Edwin would be the un-cool one, but for right then the world was spinning exactly as it always had, and this was about as wrong as wrong gets when you are ten.

"Oh look! He's here!" my mother squealed. I was dying of embarrassment as she opened the screen door and screamed out, "Noah will be right out, Edwin." Edwin said nothing and just looked up at my mom with a comatose look on his face as if he was about to do community service hours by picking up trash along the highway in an orange jumpsuit. I cringed and flinched and couldn't help but yank myself away as she tried yet again to straighten a collar that wasn't there. I felt bad because it startled her and caused her to jump. I sighed, frustrated. I picked up the pool bag and pushed open the screen door. She stood there waiting for a goodbye hug that wasn't coming. Again, I felt bad for her but worse for me.

"I have good feelings about this," she said, much too perkily and loud enough for Edwin to hear. I didn't bother looking up to see his surely rolling eyes. I walked down to the street and joined him on the sidewalk.

"Hi," I said.

"Hi," he grunted.

I guess I should have thanked him for taking me, but that would have only been embarrassing for both of us. For a couple of minutes my mind raced. Should I attempt to make small talk with him about school or church or sports or TV? But I decided against it, knowing that what Edwin really wanted was for me to be swallowed up by the sidewalk. Every once in a while I glanced up at his face which was a good six inches higher than mine. He had already filled out across the chest, and he had a very fine mustache across his lip. I wondered if he shaved. I guess when God hands out the parts, they come all in one package. I was six inches shorter, no chest, and not so much as fuzz on my lip. I wondered what it might be like to be him. I was sure it was a whole lot different than it was to be me. Even at that young age, even though I was a little different, I knew that I didn't want to be Edwin or anyone else. I liked being me. I couldn't help but notice that even his pool stuff was cooler. His goggles were already slung around his neck, and his pool bag had pictures of bleeding skulls that would make lunch out of the fish on mine.

The community pool was six streets away. At about three streets away, Edwin stopped suddenly in his tracks, turned, and looked at me. It took me a few seconds to notice that he had stopped, so when I did, I was slightly ahead of him. I turned and faced him. His face was deadly serious. "Look," he said in a warning tone, "over there is my best friend's house. We're picking him up next. You can walk to the pool with us, but when we get there, we don't know you, and you don't know us. Got it?" He stared hard at me. I nodded. He began to walk again, and I began to walk beside him.

After about three more houses, I was the one who stopped and turned to face him. I swallowed, gathering my courage. "How about we make this easier," I said, reaching into the pool bag. Unzipping the inner pocket, I took out the three dollars of snack money and held it out to him. "I won't tell my mother if you won't tell yours." His eyes lit up at the sight of the money.

Then he looked at me warily through nasty slits. "Every day?" he clarified.

"Every day." I agreed.

"Deal!" he bellowed with a grin and put his hand up for a "high five" that I didn't bother returning. He took the money and, laughing, slid it into his pocket. I heard him chuckling and muttering the word "cool" to himself as he continued down the street without me. Two houses further, a stocky, red-haired boy ran out to meet him. They fell in line together, walking on the sidewalk with matching strides that only best friends can have. A few moments later, I heard them break into laughter and high five each other as Edwin no doubt explained our "deal" to him. I stood on the sidewalk, watching them turn the corner. I was relieved as I slowly let the breath out of my tight chest. With Edwin gone, half of my problem was solved.

With the faint sound of the laughter still in my ears, I plopped down on the curb next to a mailbox. It was in front of a small white house, the smallest on the street. The house could almost be called rickety. It sat back several feet farther from the other houses, almost as if it might at one point have been a cottage of a larger house that was no longer there. It was a square box with a small front porch that had a white porch swing and a brown wooden rocker. The house was in need of painting, especially around the few square windows that dotted the front. Although it was in need of repair, the little house was kept up enough that I could tell that someone lived there, perhaps someone sad and lonely. I positioned my back against the bottom of the mailbox post for support. I didn't have a watch but guessed that by now it must be about 10:00. The pool was open until 3:00, so I figured I had about five hours to kill. I had no idea how I was going to do it, but I didn't care. I was not with Edwin and I was not at the pool, and that was all that mattered.

Next to listening to music, my second favorite thing to do was daydream. So, lazily I began to wonder about the people who lived on the street. I spent some time studying each of the houses, imagining who might live there. I loved doing this, especially on vacation when we passed through farm towns, because I knew that their lives were completely different than mine. When we would drive through, I would wonder who lived in the houses that we passed and what their lives were like. What did they do everyday? Were they happy? Did they have secrets? Sitting there I began to wonder about the people on this street. I figured their lives were more similar to mine since we lived in the same town. I guessed which houses had kids by who had swing sets in the backyard. I figured in the houses with no cars in the driveway lived people who were at work. I wondered if the people who had cars in the driveway worked at night or didn't have jobs at all. I wondered if someone who had four or five newspapers scattered on the walkway was on vacation or if maybe there was an old person inside who couldn't get down the steps to get them. I wondered if there was someone checking on them. I wondered if the folks in the houses that had lawns that had been allowed to grow too high were waiting for their grown kids to come home and cut them on the weekend. I wondered if the sight of just one of the houses was the best sight that someone had ever seen. Was it their home and safe haven? Was it someone else's childhood home that held their best memories? Was one of the homes grandma and grandpap's house and the best place to visit on Sunday for dinner? Then I even wondered if one of the houses was a place that someone hated calling home and was counting the days until they could move out.

I leaned back again on the post of the mailbox and worked on a chorus of a song that I had been secretly writing in my room at night. I played the notes of the songs on my thighs using them as my pretend keyboard. I pulled blades of grass and blew through them, trying to make a loud, shrill sound as I had seen other kids do. I found a dandelion and pulled the thin yellow petals playing "she loves me, she loves me not," except that I played "gold or platinum," to the question of whether my first album would go platinum or just gold. After about a hundred petals, I determined that I was only going gold. I shrugged and decided that this simply meant that my second album would go platinum. I don't know how long I had been sitting out on the curb, but it was broiling hot. I was sweating like crazy and was amusing myself by popping the tar bubbles that were forming from the heat on the road with a stick. I had just stuck my head inside of the top of my tee shirt to wipe the sweat off of my face when a booming voice made me jump out of my skin.

"If you're going to sit here much longer, you'll be needing to pay rent," the voice said. I popped my head out and found myself looking up at the most gigantic black man I had ever seen in all of my ten years. Not only was he the tallest man I had ever seen, but he was stocky, with legs and arms like tree trunks. After freezing from fear for a second, I awkwardly tried to scramble to my feet. I fell back twice before I actually made it upright.

"I . . . I . . . I'm sorry," I stuttered. "I can move."

"You don't need to move," he answered. "You need to pay rent." It took me a second to see the small smile cross his face. I breathed again. "Maybe you just need to introduce yourself before you go planting yourself in someone's front yard."

I gulped and nodded, knowing that I should speak but could not. He put his giant hand out for me to shake. I did. My small hand was swallowed in his.

"Good, firm handshake," he announced with what looked to be a hint of another smile. "So far, you're not bad."

I just nodded, embarrassed.

"Do you know what the temperature needs to be out here for the tar to bubble?" I shook my head no. "At least eighty-nine degrees," he said matter-of-factly. "And that's hot especially when you're just sitting here for so long. That kid who wasn't your friend dumped you here almost four hours ago. It's two o'clock." I was surprised that I had been able to kill that much time already. "Shove down," he ordered and robotically collapsed his huge frame so that he was sitting on the sidewalk. "Sit," he ordered me. "Too hot for standing." Folding himself into a seated position didn't look easy, and he kind of reminded me of a transformer. When he was sitting and I was standing, we were almost eye to eye. He was dressed in blue jean overalls and a white tee shirt. When he stretched out his huge arm, a blue-green tattoo with the names "Ruby and Lilac" in a curly cursive script was revealed.

"Stand if you want to, but you'll be more comfortable if you sit." I sat. I watched as he unwrapped from paper towels two large hard rolls stuffed with cheese. He handed one to me. My mouth watered. I hadn't realized how hungry I was. From a paper sack he pulled two bottles of root beer. He bit the cap off of his bottle and took a swallow. Then he handed me mine. "Now it's two o'clock, but lunch is at twelve everyday," he said, almost with a warning tone in his voice. "I only made an exception today because I wasn't sure if you were staying for lunch. But every other day lunch is at twelve, exactly. Got it?"

I nodded meekly. His big voice seemed to somehow use up all of the air and make me unable to talk. "Got it," I finally managed almost in a whisper.

He nodded to the sandwich. "Thank the Lord and take a bite."

I did both. I didn't realize how hungry I was until I bit into it. The roll was crusty and hard, just how I liked it. I had to use all of my teeth to yank the bread apart. The cheese was warm and a little melted. I took huge bites, and it was gone in a minute. I looked at the bottle of root beer. I had never bit the cap off of a bottle before, but that's how he got his off so I tried with mine. Once, twice, and three times I tried, until he took the bottle out of my hand and snapped off the lid with his own teeth and laughed a big laugh that came from his belly. He handed the bottle back to me.

"You'll get it by the end of the summer," he said. I wondered why he thought we would know each other at the end of the summer. I took a huge swallow. "So we shared a meal, and I'm charging you rent, and we haven't even properly introduced ourselves. Don't hardly seem right, does it?" he asked.

"No," I agreed.

"My name is Rupert Holmes," he said, holding his hand out for another shake.

"My name is Noah Jacob," I said, making sure this time that I did have a firm grip.

He reached over and clinked his root beer bottle against mine. I smiled at this. He laughed. "Well, it's nice to meet you, Noah Jacob."

"It's nice to meet you, Rupert Holmes," I said, hoping that he knew that I really meant it. I was hoping that maybe I had found a friend. I liked him.

He was looking down the street. "Well, it looks like you're leaving." My heart sank. I thought he was kicking me out already. He motioned down the street with his head. I looked up to see Edwin and his friend making their way back down the street towards us. My stomach hurt at the sight of them. I knew I had to walk back home with them if I was going to convince my mother that I really was at the pool. I nodded.

Rupert gathered up the paper towels and the root beer bottles. "See you tomorrow, Noah Jacob," as he unfolded himself and picked himself up off of the sidewalk. He turned and walked back to the house. He had left the bottle caps lying there so I picked them up off the sidewalk and put them in my pocket. I stood up when Edwin and his friend came closer, picked up my bag, and fell in line behind them. They said nothing at first and didn't acknowledge me until we were about three houses away.

"So you met Mr. Holmes?" Edwin said with a surly smile on his face. I nodded. "No, you didn't," he said leaning grossly into me with rotten, bad breath. "You met a big, good-for-nothing, dumb, old black man," he said, laughing with the meanest smile I had ever seen on anyone's face.

I was instantly filled with disgust and anger and did something without hesitation that I had never in my life felt I had to do before. I made a fist, the fist that my dad had made me practice a bunch of times one night in our living room when I was in kindergarten and a kid named Curtis wouldn't stop picking on me. I curled my fingers up around my balled up palm and planted my fist right in the middle of

Edwin's face. "No," I said with a calm that I never knew I possessed. "I met Mr. Rupert Holmes."

I waited for the pounding that I was sure was coming from Edwin and his friend, but instead all they did was stare at me, wide-eyed and confused. It was the hardest punch I knew how to throw, and to be honest Edwin seemed less fazed by the punch itself than by the fact that I had thrown it at all. Edwin's friend looked back and forth between the two of us so fast, from one of our faces to the other, waiting for something to happen, that it was like he was watching a tennis match on TV. But nothing did happen.

With an almost confused look on his face Edwin said, "I wouldn't do that again, kid." I said nothing. Then for good measure he added, "All I gotta say is you better have snack money tomorrow." Then he turned around and started back down the street. The friend looked at me, wide-eyed, one more time. Then I guess, as a gesture of loyalty to Edwin, he shot me a glare and said, "Yeah." He turned and fell in perfect stride alongside Edwin. I followed a few paces behind them the whole way home, wondering just what this summer would bring.

Checkers

At ten o'clock the next morning I walked out my front door with my pool bag in my hand and my mother waving to me from the porch. She had pumped me endlessly the night before at dinner as to how my day at the pool had gone. I supplied her with all of the right answers. She would have kept fishing for details but, thankfully, my father made her stop. I assured her as best I could that it had gone fine. I felt a little bad lying to her but justified it in my mind by telling myself that the time I did spend with Edwin went as well as it could have.

That second day, I met Edwin on the sidewalk, and wordlessly we walked the few blocks with him in front and me trailing behind. When we got to Rupert's house, he turned to face me. He glared and held out his hand. I unzipped the inner pocket of the pool bag, took out the snack money, and handed it to him. I felt guilty seeing that on his right cheek there was a small, reddish-purple mark beneath his eye that I was pretty sure I had made. As Edwin continued down the street, I stood in front of Rupert's house, not exactly sure what I was supposed to do. The day before he spoke of me coming back, but I wasn't sure if he meant it or not. Just because I was welcome yesterday didn't mean for sure that I was welcome today. But he did take the time to tell me that lunch was at twelve o'clock sharp. I played all this back and forth in my mind, but decided either way—even if I spent the rest of the day, the rest of the summer, sitting on the curb—I was at least free of Edwin, his friends, and the pool. I was even free of everyone else who would be wondering why I wanted to be in my bedroom singing the soundtrack to *West Side Story* instead of something more acceptably "normal" like going to the pool or playing ball in the street. It was a summer day and I was free, and I was ten years old, and that was not a bad place to be.

I stood scanning the street up and down. It was perfectly still. The fact that it was already broiling hot somehow made it feel even more still. Rupert's house was still also. There was no sign of him. So I sat down next to the mailbox with my back resting on the post, just like the day before. Suddenly a booming voice startled me out of my skin.

"You can come as far as the porch," the voice bellowed. It was Rupert's voice, and it was coming from the porch but I still couldn't see him. I stood up and walked cautiously toward the house. As I gingerly stepped onto the whitewashed wooden porch, I saw him sitting in a brown wooden rocker that was hidden by a huge lilac bush growing in front of the right side of the porch.

"Hi," I said, stepping up timidly.

"Good morning, Noah Jacob," Rupert said. "You can come as far as the porch today. I haven't for sure figured out yet if you're some kind of criminal or not, so I can't be letting you into my house." I nodded in agreement.

"Sit," he commanded. I went over to the only other seat on the porch, which was the white wooden swing hanging at the opposite end. I didn't know it then, but that swing would be my seat for the summer. I climbed on. The chains that held it creaked a bit, but I was small and short, so I knew it would hold me. I wondered how long it had been since anyone had sat on it. The paint was peeling, and it scratched the bare legs around my shorts. I faced Rupert, and Rupert faced me.

We sat in silence for a few moments, then leaning back in his rocker and taking a suck on his pipe, Rupert said, "You know, when two people are trying to get to know each other, it doesn't always take a lot of words. You'd be surprised at how much you can get to know a person with just a few words." I nodded. I didn't know exactly what he meant, but I was interested. "Actually," he continued, rising from his chair, retrieving a box containing a checker board and checkers from a side table, "A person can learn all he needs to learn about a person in just one checker game." He opened the box and began to set it up on a table between the two of us. I kind of doubted him on this but tried not to let it show. He easily read my face. "Doubting, heh?" he asked. My face flushed. "Yeah," he said again. "People aren't half as complicated as they like to think they are." The game was set up. I was black, and he was red. He pulled his rocker a bit closer and looked me square in the eyes, putting one finger on a checker piece. He said, "My name is Rupert, Rupert Holmes," then slid the piece forward.

I froze for a moment, knowing that it was my turn. But, pretty sure I knew what to do, I placed my own finger on one of my checkers. I responded, "My name is Noah, Noah Jacob," and slid my piece into place.

Rupert nodded like he was impressed. Then ready for his next move, he said, "Son of Rupert, son of Sadie." He slid the checker.

"Son of George, son of Angelina," I responded with a move.

"Louisiana," he said emphatically, leaning back in his chair a bit.

I had to think about this one for a moment, then I realized that he was giving me his birth place. "Utah," I countered with a move of my own. He nodded. I smiled, proud that I had figured this out.

"Edgar, William, Mary Rose, and Violet," he said and slid a checker further on to my side of the board. I had to think for a moment but got it quickly. These were his siblings.

"Dina, Colin, Gracie, and Molly," I said and slid a checker.

Rupert nodded like he was planning strategy. Then shaking his head back and forth and licking his lips he closed his eyes and gushed, "Jambalaya and root beer."

I laughed. This one was fun. "Spaghetti and meatballs," I answered, moving a checker.

Next, he curled up his nose and said, "Spinach," and moved a checker.

I laughed, curled up my nose and said, "Peas," and moved a checker.

"Fishing and rocking," he said with a slide.

"Climbing trees and go-karting," I smiled, making a move while envisioning my favorite things.

"Music," Rupert said surely.

"Music," I answered just as surely.

"Singing," he offered, maneuvering a checker.

"Singing," I agreed, moving one of my own.

"God," he said firmly with a finality in his voice.

"God," I replied just as surely.

I was waiting for more, until I looked up and found Rupert resting back in his rocker with a teasing grin on his face. I looked down on the checker board to discover that he had cleared the board of all of my checkers and had won the game while I had not captured a single one of his checkers. I had been so busy concentrating on my answers that I forgot to play the game too. He threw his head back and laughed a huge belly laugh. I put my hands over my eyes, embarrassed, which made him laugh louder. In a moment we were laughing together. Right then I knew that this was going to be a good summer. Rupert Holmes was one cool guy.

"Lunch time," Rupert announced rising from his chair. I couldn't tell if the creaking sounds that I heard were from his old bones or the old rocker. He ambled toward the door and, as he reached out toward the screen door to open it, I again caught sight of the tattoo reading the names "Ruby and Lilac."

I waited outside on the porch swing, kicking it back and forth with the toe of my sneaker that was just barely able to touch the floor every other kick. After a few minutes Rupert returned with my root beer and my cheese sandwich. I had been hoping it would be the same as the day before.

"Thank the Lord and eat, Noah Jacob," he ordered. I obeyed. When we were done, we sat in a comfortable silence.

"Well, I think that we have finally been officially introduced," Rupert said. I smiled in agreement.

I couldn't help but notice that our last lines were exactly the same—the lines that spoke of loving God. I told Rupert this. "That makes us alike," I said proudly.

"Yes, I do agree it does. It makes us both Believers," he said lighting up his pipe. "It makes us both Believers." I laid back on the swing smiling, replaying his words in my head.

Then, suddenly, I thought of something. "Rupert, who," I asked, "are Ruby and Lilac?" I watched as his peaceful face saddened. I became afraid that I had asked the wrong question, one that made him angry or hurt him. My eyes started to sting as I saw the saddest look on his face. I stopped holding my breath when he finally spoke.

"Tomorrow," he said very softly. "I'll tell you tomorrow." I nodded, still studying him.

"Looks like it's time for you to go anyway," he said quietly and motioned to Edwin and his friend waiting for me at the end of the walk.

I nodded and got up. "See you tomorrow, Rupert," I said, getting up from the swing.

"See you tomorrow, Noah," he said. I walked down the steps and started down the street, only looking back once to see his face, finding that he looked almost like himself again, but not quite.

Ruby and Lilac

Edwin was late meeting me, so I was late for Rupert. He was sitting on the wooden rocker on the front porch when I hopped up. "I was fearing you weren't coming," he said. I loved that he said that.

"Naaa," I assured him. "I'll always come." It felt good that someone somewhere was waiting for me.

Rupert was busy whittling something out of a piece of wood with a knife. He handed me a plain bar of white soap and a plastic knife. I looked at them blankly. "Get to whittling," he said.

"I don't know how to whittle," I objected.

"Get to whittling," he repeated as if I hadn't said a word. That was one thing about Rupert—he wasn't big on excuses.

"You're ten years old," he told me. "You can do anything. It's one of the prizes of being ten. All of the doors are open."

Obediently, I began to whittle away at the soft piece of soap. I had no idea what I was making, but I liked the way the shavings curled off of the soap when I manipulated the knife in just the right way. We sat together and whittled in a comfortable silence. At that point we hadn't known each other for very long, but somehow it felt much longer. Sometimes we talked, sometimes we didn't, but it never felt awkward.

The question that I asked him the day before about Ruby and Lilac was gnawing at me, but as badly as I wanted to know, and as young and anxious as I was, I knew about overstepping the bounds. But I did want to know who Ruby and Lilac were. Somehow I knew that if I knew the story of Ruby and Lilac then I would know Rupert. And I was right.

Every once in a while, I looked up at him when I thought he wasn't looking and studied his face. I did that a lot. I memorized every single line of his seventy-eight year old face. I liked the way Rupert's face was wrinkly and hoped that when I was his age, mine would be wrinkly too. It looked neat to me. I'm not exactly sure how to describe it, but somehow it seemed that his wrinkly face proudly showed people that he had lived a good long time. Every once in while he would look down at me, his eyes peering over or under his taped-together reading glasses. After about an hour of silent whittling and me sneaking peeks at him, he cleared his throat and said, in a very serious tone, "If you don't ask me, then I won't tell you."

My cheeks flushed as I realized he could read my mind. I took a deep breath and softly said, "Who are Ruby and Lilac?" I asked quietly, just barely loud enough for him to hear me. For a few moments he was silent.

"I will tell you once and only once," he said firmly. "I'll tell you total and complete. No questions," he further warned. "Then we never speak of them again. Understand?" He asked seriously. I nodded solemnly, with my eyes glued to his face, realizing that this was an honor. I knew that maybe I should look down at my whittling to make the telling more comfortable for him, but I couldn't. I was afraid that by looking away, I would somehow miss a word. And I knew that I was about to hear an amazing story that I would never forget. Rupert took one deep breath then told me the saddest story that I would ever hear in my entire life.

He began with a question that took me off guard. "How many black people besides me live on this side of town?" he asked. I froze, knowing that the answer was none but wasn't sure that I should say that I knew that. But everyone knew that Rupert was the only black person on this side of town. The black community lived on the other side of town. I shrugged. He looked up over his glasses with a look that told me that I was not getting away with that as an answer.

"None," I said.

"Right," he answered. "Did you ever wonder why?"

I shook my head because I actually never had.

"Because I couldn't leave," he said. "Because this is where my loves are. This is where my Ruby and my Lilac are."

For the next two hours I lay on the floor of the porch whittling and listening to how Rupert Holmes came to be in Utah. Fifty-eight years earlier, Rupert travelled to Rankin, Utah, for what he thought was a three-month job. He was twenty years old and already married to his wife, Ruby, and a father to his daughter, Lilac, who he said was the single most important thing he ever did in his life. He could have left them with his parents in Louisiana, but he loved them too much to do that. He simply didn't want to be apart from them. Rupert said that even his family criticized him for it, saying, "A man goes off to work, and a woman stays home and tends to the house and children." He said that Ruby was a dutiful wife and would have done whatever he said. But he was the one who didn't want to be apart from them, no matter what people said. In his mind a good man kept his family together.

Rupert laughed out loud when he told me of how she had jumped for glee, throwing herself into his arms when he told her to pack what little they had because he was taking them with him.

When they finally reached Rankin, after a the long difficult train ride in a luggage car of a train from Louisiana, they arrived on the very plot of land that we were on, to work for the rich man who worked in the big house. I realized that what I suspected was right, that there was once a bigger house in front of this one. Rupert said that it was the biggest house on the street, the most beautiful Victorian house he had ever seen. The factory owner who he had come to work for lived in it. Rupert said that the big house had burned to the ground years ago, never to be built again, leaving the small house. I realized that was why Rupert's house looked out of place and odd on the street as it was presently. All the others that still stood were main houses with the servant's houses having been torn down years before.

When the factory owner saw that Rupert showed up in Utah with his wife and daughter, he was at first annoyed, then strangely touched when he asked Rupert why he would do a hare-brained thing like hauling his wife and child out west for such a short time instead of leaving them back home. Rupert simply answered, "A good man keeps his family together." The rich factory owner liked Rupert immediately and offered him the shed to stay in. So while Rupert went off to work eighteen hours a day at the rich man's factory. Ruby and Lilac stayed back, making the shed a home.

Rupert said he remembered the day like it was yesterday. It was a grueling, broiling hot Tuesday, early in the afternoon. The hundred or so factory men were working steadily like a machine, each doing his part, when something changed. Finding the right words to describe what changed the mood and aura was impossible. Rupert said that it felt as if even the air had changed and that it was somehow growing more still and impossibly cooler, like something bad creeping in. Of course, there was no PA system back then, so the only way to get messages from man to man was by word of mouth, and in the noisy factory this meant yelling from man to man. Rupert said that he heard the faint calling from one man to another and listened as it grew louder, but at first paid it no attention because the men often goofed off like this to break the boredom. But then, somewhere in the cacophony of yelling men and clanking machinery, he could make out the faint calling of his own name. He stopped his work and listened, and—sure enough— he heard his name making its way closer and closer to him. But they were saying something after his name that he couldn't quite make out yet. But on the third listen he got it. They were shouting from one to another, "Rupert Holmes! You gotta get home!" Rupert said he must have been in some kind of shock because he stood frozen until the guy next to him walked over and literally shook him and shouted "Rupert Holmes. You gotta get home!"

Paralyzed no longer, he took off at a run, knowing that something had to be terribly, horribly wrong at home. He ran the fastest three miles a man could possibly run, all the way back to the shed, with his head swimming with endless horrifying scenarios. When he got there, he first ran through the front door of the house, screaming Ruby and Lilac's names. Room to room he ran finding neither of them. But when he busted out the back screen door, almost tearing it off its hinges, he saw her, knowing that sometimes in life just one snapshot, one image in your head, one blink, can tell you exactly what has happened, what is wrong, what will never be right, and what will change your life forever.

What Rupert saw was his wife, Ruby, lying at the edge of the pond in the back yard. She was in the fetal position, wearing her pink and blue rose print dress, rocking back and forth, wailing. Her face was buried in her hands. He knew instantly that Lilac was in the pond, at the bottom of the pond. Rupert barely noticed the few neighbors—the white ladies from the houses around and a couple of their husbands who had gathered. Every once in a while one of them would try to approach Ruby, but she would react by raising one arm and swatting them away. They all stood paralyzed, unable to help her, but unable to leave her, too. Rupert nodded to each of them in thanks as if to say, "I'll handle it from here."

One by one, not knowing what else to do, they began to leave. The ladies said nothing, wiping their sweating brows and dabbing their eyes with handkerchiefs as they walked back to their own homes. A couple of the men approached Rupert and offered a hand to shake. Graciously, he obliged. The other men just walked away, shaking their heads.

Rupert tried to approach Ruby with a soft word and a gentle touch, but she swatted him away just as she had the strangers, almost as if she didn't recognize him or his voice. Ruby wailed Lilac's name again and again, rocking back and forth for hours. Rupert stopped trying to approach her and instead just sat on the grass next to her as close as she would allow. The sun slipped lower in the sky until it disappeared completely into the pitch black night. Because she was finally exhausted from wailing and crying, Rupert was able to pick up the crumpled body of his broken wife and carry her into the house. As they crossed the threshold of the doorway back into the house, Ruby muttered some of the few words she ever spoke after that, "Rupert, she's afraid of the dark."

"I know," Rupert managed, pushing back her matted hair. "I know."

My eyes were glued to Rupert. I couldn't help it. I wasn't sure if I should ask, but I had to. "What happened to Ruby?" I asked in a whisper.

Rupert told me that he put her in their bed that night, and for the remaining months of his stay at that job she never got out of it. Rupert went to work every day and came home every night, and she wouldn't have moved out of that bed. At first, while he was at work, the neighbor ladies tried to nurse her back, but she refused their company. They stopped coming, and instead Rupert would come home to a pot of soup or a casserole set by the front door. Rupert spent the evenings trying to nurse Ruby as well as packing up the house. The time of the job was ending, and the night before his last day of work the three boxes that contained every possession they had stood packed and ready by the door. He would work his last day, then they would start back to Louisiana. He told all of this to Ruby like he told her everything, in a soothing, calm voice. In return, he got what he always got—a completely blank stare from dark eyes that used to be Ruby's bright, glowing ones. She hadn't spoken in two months except to mutter an inaudible, "Good mothers don't leave their babies."

On the last day of the job, Rupert came home and walked through the front door. The house was cooler than it should have been—that was the first sign that something again was very wrong. He realized the back kitchen door was wide open and that the air was blowing from front to back. He darted out the back door. This time he did not find Ruby in front of the pond. This time, like before, he saw a snapshot that told him the entire story. This time he found only a dress—Ruby's dress, the blue one with the pink roses that she had refused to take off since the day that they lost Lilac in the pond. Rupert knew immediately what she had done. He could picture her in his mind walking to the edge of the pond, slipping her tiny frame out of the dress, and walking directly into the water to be with her child. Rupert walked to the pond, picked up the dress, and folded it neatly. He took it back into the house and hung it in the closet.

The owner of the factory came by later that night to tell Rupert that he was welcome to stay on at the factory and live in the shed for as long as he liked. Rupert thanked him and told him, "A good man keeps his family together."

After Rupert finished talking, all I could do was stare at him.

Rupert said nothing else. The story was over. He got up from the rocker and went into the house. He came back a few minutes later with lunch. He handed me my sandwich and bit the caps off of both bottles and handed one to me. Like always, I scooped up the caps and stuck them in my pocket. We ate our lunch in silence.

After lunch, Rupert got up and wordlessly walked around the house to the pond. I quickly got up and followed him. As he rounded the side of the house, he pulled a lilac blossom from the bush that had grown so big that it nearly covered one side of the house. Rupert told me, "The entire time Ruby was birthing Lilac the sweet smell of lilacs from the open window at her momma's house kept her going. That is why we named her Lilac."

Rupert walked to the pond and sat his big lumbering body down on its edge. I sat down beside him. "That is why we never go into the pond or throw rocks into it, Noah Jacob." I nodded, knowing that he used my full name for a reason. I understood.

I watched as Rupert pulled one petal at a time off the large lilac blossom that he had picked and set it gently on the edge of the water. Together we watched as the wind took the petal from the edge into the middle. It swirled it around for awhile then gently took it under. It looked pretty and peaceful to me.

I wondered if I dared do something that I was thinking. I wasn't sure if it was the right or wrong thing. But I decided that maybe Rupert would take it for exactly what I meant. I fished the soap that I had whittled out of the pocket of my jeans. I had whittled the soap into the shape of a cross. I remembered from science class that soap floats. Rupert watched me. I kissed the cross ever so gently, laid down on my stomach and, reaching as far as I could, I set it into the edge of the water. Together we watched as the wind took it away and in abstract lines floated it around the pond. The reflection of the sun bouncing off of the glistening white soap looked pretty. At first I didn't dare look up at Rupert, but I did timidly when I heard him say, "Thank you, Noah Jacob." My heart swelled. I had done the right thing.

"You're welcome, Rupert," I said.

We sat together by the pond until three o'clock and it was time for me to go. I reached over and touched Rupert on the shoulder as I walked away, leaving him by the glistening pond.

Saint and Angels

I was lying on the living room floor of Rupert's house on my back with my arms stretched high in the air. I wiggled my fingers, playing with the dust and rainbow reflections that were coming through the front window panes. It was a Friday about two weeks after we had met each other. So far we had spent our days together leisurely. Sometimes we did odd jobs that needed doing—fixing leaky faucets or tightening loose drain pipes or painting rusty railings. Rupert was different than most adults. He didn't just have me stand by him, holding the tools or watching, but instead he actually had me do the work. He showed me how to maneuver the screwdriver just right and how to paint without leaving swirls. He told me to never forget that most problems in the world could be fixed with duct tape. He'd started letting me into the house on the third day after we met, announcing that he had determined that I was neither a murderer nor a thief and, besides that, it was too hot out on the porch for him.

"Can't be too careful sizing people up, Mr. Jacob," he warned me. "There are a lot of wolves in sheep clothing out there."

"What do you mean?" I asked him.

"I mean that just because you look harmless like a scrawny little white boy doesn't mean that you are."

"Are what? I asked.

"A scrawny, harmless-looking white boy" he said.

I mulled this over. "What am I then?" I asked.

Then he laughed, "A scrawny, harmless, little white boy." His laughter came from deep inside.

Rupert was rocking back and forth in his rocking chair, sucking on his pipe, and trying to read the newspaper while I was chattering at him on the floor. "Let's play the Crystal Ball Game," I suggested.

Rupert grunted over the newspaper, "I'm not a big fan of this game," he reminded.

"I know," I began to plead, "but I'll be reasonable." I promised.

He looked at me skeptically. "You never are. But give it a try," he conceded.

The Crystal Ball Game was a game that I had made up. In it, I asked Rupert random questions about me and him, the future and actually anything else I could think of, and he had to answer them like he knew. The rule was that he couldn't say, "I don't know." He had to answer just as if he was looking into a crystal ball.

I started off with simple questions about some of my concerns. "Will I get Mrs. Romo or Mr. Harris for sixth grade?"

"Mrs. Romo," he answered, fast and sure like he actually knew. For me, that is what made the game so fun, pretending to really know the future.

"Will I have a cool car when I'm sixteen?"

"Absolutely."

"What color will it be?"

"Red."

"Will I need braces?"

"Need, no. Get, yes. Your mother will insist."

"Will I get married?"

"For sure."

"Favorites!!" I announced, abruptly changing the subject. "Blue or green?"

"Blue."

"Corvettes or Jaguars?"

"Jaguars."

"Snow or rain?"

"Snow."

"Being a policeman or a fireman?"

"Policeman."

"Eating fried worms or grasshoppers dipped in mud?"

Rupert looked up over the top of his newspaper, warning, "You're losing me."

"Choose," I giggled.

"The worms," he sighed. A seventy-eight-year-old man could only have so much patience for a ten-year-old comedian.

"Hanging off a cliff only wearing your underwear or walking through the mall in a bikini?"

"Done" Rupert shouted, slamming his newspaper shut.

"OK, OK," I laughed hysterically, rolling around on the floor. "Just pick, please," I begged.

"The mall," he said, shaking his head and swatting me with the rolled-up newspaper.

"Kissing your grandmother on the mouth or a gorilla on the butt?" I shouted, laughing hard and trying to get one more question in.

"Game over!" Rupert bellowed.

I giggled to myself for a while, then stayed quiet, day-dreaming more questions in my head as Rupert took another try at the sports page. After a couple of minutes I said, "Just one more?"

"Nope," he said.

"Please," I begged.

"Nope," he said again.

"Pretty please?" I pleaded, staring at him while he was trying to read, knowing that no one can read with someone staring at them.

He looked up at me with a warning look and said, "One more."

"When we get to heaven, if we get the chance to pick, will you pick to be an angel or a saint?"

For a minute he said nothing, then he put down the newspaper and took off his glasses and looked at me. I think I may have seen a small smile cross his face, but I wasn't sure. After a minute of silence, I knew that he was taking my question seriously.

"I believe I will pick being a saint," he said. "Yeah, yeah, for sure," he answered more decisively. "A saint."

"Saint Rupert. That sounds good," I nodded. "Saints always have powers," I told him. "What power would you pick to have to help people?"

He thought for only a minute. "Relieving guilt," he said finally. "I would relieve guilt."

He didn't have to say it, but I knew this had a lot to do with how he felt about what happened to Ruby and Lilac. I was young, but I knew that he probably wrongly blamed himself for what happened to them.

"What would you pick?" he asked me. "A saint or an angel?"

I rolled over and propped my head in my hands. "Saints are cool," I reasoned. "And I used to always think that I would pick a saint because I like the idea of helping people, but I would want my power to be that I was stretchy, and I'm not exactly sure how I could help people with my stretchy power."

Rupert had a big smile on his face by this time and had given up on his newspaper and was just listening to me. "I'm not sure either," he said, not even trying to act serious.

"But I changed my mind," I told him. "I definitely will pick angel because I totally want to fly."

Rupert just laughed out loud.

"Don't laugh," I ordered, laughing myself.

"No. No," he said still chuckling. "Wanting to fly is reasonable," he said. "Flying would be good."

"Flying would be super cool," I corrected. "The only reason I ever really considered being a saint anyway is because it seems as if they always make angels wear all white and I was thinking that might be embarrassing."

I expected him to laugh, but instead he just smiled down at me, and said, "It will be your heaven. God will work with you on the color."

I nodded, never having thought of this. It would be my heaven, so who knows? "Definitely angel," I said to myself firmly, glad to have it decided.

"Angel Noah," Rupert smiled.

"Saint Rupert," I said back. We smiled at each other. "Do you think I'll make a good one?" I asked him.

"I know you will," he said, folding up the newspaper and putting his eyeglasses back in their case. "I'll tell you one more thing I know," he announced, pulling his creaky body up from the rocker. "School should be all year long."

"No way!" I wailed.

"Yes way!" he wailed, mocking me.

"Why?" I asked, exasperated.

"Because you should be learning instead of playing with dust at my house."

I was offended.

"You should be learning," he repeated, walking across the room. I followed him. "And you will be," he said surely.

"What do you mean?" I asked warily.

He laughed because he knew he had me scared. "Starting Monday, you're going to the School of Rupert Holmes," he announced in his big, loud, playful voice.

"Wait a minute," I protested, walking so close behind him that I bumped into him. He chuckled, ignoring me. He was enjoying this.

"Bring your brain and your walking shoes," he instructed.

I just stared at him, wondering what in the world he meant. "I don't know about this," I protested again.

"I do," he said firmly. "I know one more thing, too," he said.

"What?" I asked him suspiciously.

"It's time for you to go," he laughed, pushing me across the room and through the front screen door, motioning to Edwin and his friend waiting for me on the sidewalk. My mouth was still hanging open as I reached the sidewalk. I watched as Rupert walked back into his house out of view, calling over his shoulder, "Your brain and your walking shoes!"

Then I heard him laughing.

The Believers

"So you came back, did you?" Rupert grinned as I walked in the door the next Monday. "I was afraid you might not want to go to the School of Rupert Holmes."

"I don't," I admitted, still nervous as to what all of this was about. "But what choice do I have?"

"You could go to the pool," Rupert teased, knowing that I'd rather die. "Still not too late," he chided, motioning to Edwin and his friend making their way down the street. "Looks like the train hasn't completely pulled away yet." I just gave him a look which caused him to laugh heartily.

"So you're not moving. So I guess you're staying at school," he laughed. I sighed.

"Why can't we just hang around like always?" I whined.

"Purpose," Rupert answered firmly. "Purpose. God gives everyone a purpose, and I do believe that He didn't just drop you on my doorstep by chance. He dropped you for a purpose. And I have come to believe that somewhere in seventy-eight-year-old me there is some teaching He wants me to do and somewhere in ten-year-old you there is some learning He wants you to do. So there you have it," he said simply. "Purpose."

I sighed, shrugged, and nodded. I was finished resisting. "What kind of school is the School of Rupert Holmes?" I asked.

"Good question," Rupert said. "But you know the answer."

I didn't know the answer and shrugged.

"What are we?" he asked. "This is old," he reminded me.

Suddenly, I did know. "Believers!" I said, excited to get the right answer.

"Believers in what?" he pressed.

"In God," I answered.

He nodded, saying, "So there you have it." The School of Rupert Holmes is a school for Believers like me and you."

"But we already believe. What's more to know?" I asked.

"Oh, you'd be surprised," he said. "So since you aren't leaving, I'm guessing we'd better be getting started."

"I am staying," I said surely. I knew even then that there was no place else on earth that I would rather be than with Rupert.

"So welcome to school," he announced in such a big radio voice that it gave me chills. I rolled my eyes. "None of that," he scolded and whacked me with the newspaper. "One lesson learned," he mumbled as he went to the book shelf that stood alongside the fireplace. He pulled out an oversized book that even he had to carry with two hands. I could tell no one had looked at it for awhile because of the dust that had collected on it. On the cover were the words, "Religions of the World," imprinted in a simple style in faded gold foil. The rest of the book cover was a worn burgundy leather. He leafed through the book and, when he found what he was looking for, he handed it to me and said, "Give this a read."

Opening the book to the page that he had marked, I saw the words, "The Catholic Church," printed at the top. There were about six paragraphs about the church with a black and white photograph of a church and a picture of the pope. I began to read it to myself.

"Aloud," he scolded. "Clear and loud."

I only read a few more words, and he became frustrated. He looked around the room frantically. "Here," he said and pulled a blue woven rug out from under the coffee table and had me stand in the center of it. "Straight, tall, clear, and loud," he ordered.

I was beginning to think that the pool might not be so bad. But I was a good reader and read the paragraphs aloud. He nodded.

"Well, what do you think?' he asked. I shrugged.

"Sounds OK to me," I admitted.

"Me too," he agreed, like this was a reasonable thing to think.

"Are you Catholic?" he asked. I shook my head no.

I wasn't sure if I was allowed to ask him but I did, "Are you?"

"No," he said. "So why care about them Catholics?"

This felt like a disrespectfully tricky question. I knew that we shouldn't say that we shouldn't care. So I didn't say anything.

"Is God Catholic?" he asked me.

"I don't know." I laughed, thinking that this sounded kind of silly but not knowing exactly why. "Do you think He is?"

"I don't know either," he said with a look on his face that looked a whole lot like he might know.

"Well, maybe we ought to go and check this out," Rupert said as he slid off his brown leather shoes and began putting on a pair of white tennis shoes. He looked like Mr. Rogers.

"We're not going to be able to do that!" I insisted. "And you know that!"

"Not much faith going on in there," Rupert said, tapping my head. I was insulted. "It certainly can't hurt to go and talk about it," he mused. I just shook my head back and forth.

"Did you bring your walking shoes?" I looked down at my old sneakers and didn't bother telling him that no one but he had walking shoes anymore.

"Let's go," he announced. I couldn't imagine what we were going to do and was getting a little bit nervous.

"You know we won't see anybody," I told him. "It's Monday. There's nobody at church on Monday." We stepped out onto the sidewalk.

"It's the best time to catch Him," Rupert insisted. "God's always home on Monday, tired after listening to everyone on Sunday. Everyone stops by on Sunday." He winked at me. I laughed. I decided to relax and just go with it. After all, we were going on a field trip.

Rupert stood in the middle of the sidewalk getting his bearings, pointing and gazing in one direction then the other. "This way," he finally decided. "And I hope those shoes are comfortable because those Catholics are pretty far out." We were almost halfway down the street before I realized that we were actually walking all the way across town to the Catholic church.

"But no one will be there," I protested. "It's Monday."

"Who won't be there?" Rupert asked, shocked. I knew what he meant.

"I mean God will be there, of course," I said. " It's just that the Catholics won't be. You have to go on a Sunday to see one of them."

"Is that so?" Rupert laughed. "Keep walking, child, and read too," he barked. Along the way Rupert had me carry the heavy book and read more pages aloud about the Catholic church. Some of what I read I already knew; most I was learning. The heavy book made my arms ache.

"By the end of the summer that book will feel as light as feather," he told me. I didn't believe him. It was a long walk; Rupert estimated about two miles. There were five churches and one synagogue scattered in the town we lived in, dotted politely apart, not interfering with each other.

"There it is!" I said excitedly when I could see the steeple from about a block away. Rupert nodded and ambled on. He was in very good shape for a man his age, but these were long walks and occasionally we had to find a curb along the way to rest upon.

"Sure mighty pretty," he observed when we were right in front of the Catholic church. We stood surveying it up and down. It was a tall church made of large rectangular blocks with huge concrete steps that led up to the massive front door. The large cross at the top seemed a million miles high, and I swear it was touching the clouds. Rupert wiped his brow with his handkerchief, and we climbed the stairs. We pulled on the heavy wooden door and, to my surprise, it opened with a creak.

"And you thought no one would be home," he smiled and winked at me.

"I just meant it's Monday," I whispered once we were inside. "I know that He's"—I motioned upward with my head—"always home."

Rupert chuckled and motioned upward with his head, too. "Especially Mondays," he whispered with a laugh in his voice. "He's tired from all the company on Sunday. All that yapping on Sunday makes Him tired, so Monday is the best day to catch Him."

I shook my head back and forth and muffled a big laugh. I had never heard anyone talk like Rupert. But boy, did I love it. The church was still and quiet and almost dark except for the subdued glowing light that gleamed through the stained glass windows that covered almost every wall of the church. The light gave it a blue-purple glow that gave the church a cozy feel. We learned from what we read to dip one finger into the holy water, make the sign of the cross, and genuflect on one knee before sitting. We did this, then found a pew and sat down. I would have picked a pew a few rows back from the front, but Rupert said that he believed in front row seating.

Rupert knelt so I knelt, and we said quiet prayers to ourselves. I said one of the prayers that I knew from my church, hoping that it would be OK and that I wasn't offending anyone. I wondered what Rupert was thinking next to me.

Then Rupert began to talk. "Hello, Lord!" he called loudly. His voice bellowed in the empty church and echoed off the beautiful walls. I looked up at him and smiled, not exactly comfortable with him yelling in church, nervously wanting to laugh and shush him and tell him to keep going all at the same time.

"It's Rupert and Noah—your Believers. We were passing by in the neighborhood, and we thought we'd just stop and say hello just in case, well, just in case you were Catholic."

I giggled and he looked at me and winked, because this did sound a little ridiculous. "You see," Rupert explained, "we were just wanting to cover ourselves."

"Honesty is the best policy," he whispered, leaning toward me.

I wanted to tell him that since God can hear our thoughts, I was pretty sure that He could hear our whispers too, but why bother? I had no idea what to make of all of this because I had never seen anyone joke with God before like He was a friend.

"We read on the way over here, God, and learned a lot, too. You Catholics have a whole lot of nice things going on. I especially like how you honor your mother. Never can treat a good woman, especially your mom, too well," Rupert said. "Noah here"—I jumped at the sound of my name—"especially liked the candles. We have twenty-five cents, and before we leave we'll light one and you keep it burning for us. I guess we'll just be quiet for a bit more and do a touch more praying."

After a few quick minutes, Rupert said, "Well," as if we had just had pie and coffee in someone's living room and were excusing ourselves to head home. "We better be heading home. Thanks for having us." He got up and stretched his legs. I got up too and started walking back down the aisle. Halfway down the aisle Rupert turned back and commented, "Sure is a beautiful house you've got here. Mighty, mighty beautiful," he commented. I nodded in agreement. I wanted God to know that I felt the same way.

Back outside we headed down the stairs. At the bottom Rupert put his head down and was looking for something on the sidewalk and stairs. He found what he was looking for and began picking up small stones and chips of concrete from the stairs. I watched him put them in his pocket. He winked at me when he caught me watching. When I asked what they were for, he put me off and simply said that I would know "in due time."

We took turns lugging the big book back the two miles to Rupert's house. Along the way, Rupert insisted we do math problems and practice spelling words. "Just don't want your mind to go to mush is all," Rupert explained. It didn't take me long to realize that Rupert Holmes was a very smart man who knew a lot of things. By the end of the summer, I was convinced he knew everything.

By the time we got home, we were starving for lunch. The cheese sandwiches and root beer never tasted so good. After lunch, Rupert announced, "Recess!"

"You mean we're not done with school yet?" I asked.

"Recess," Rupert repeated, turning on his old rabbit-eared TV to *The Price Is Right*, his favorite show—actually the only show he ever watched. "Recess," he said again. "Then school until three."

Then he ignored me and was glued to his show. I never really watched *The Price Is Right* before meeting him. I started off not caring much for it, but by the end of the summer I swear it was my favorite show too. The most fun part for me was watching Rupert watch it. He became so involved and animated, just like people did in sporting events. He oohed and awwwed, complimented and criticized, made guesses on his own, yelled at the contestants, and encouraged Bob Barker whom he loved. *The Price Is Right* was Rupert Holmes's Super Bowl every day of the year. When the show was over, he flicked off the TV. "The other guy should have won the showcase," he muttered to himself. "Everyone knows the price of washers and dryers have gone up."

"Now what are we going to do?" I asked warily. "I think I learned enough for one day."

"Not even close," Rupert smiled. He went back to the bookcase and pulled another huge book from the shelf. As he opened it, I read the binding: *Legends of Music*. This got my attention, and I started to think that this just might not be so bad. I was right. He opened it to a section and had me stand straight and tall in the center of the round woven carpet in the middle of the living room and read about Elvis Presley. When I was done, he asked me what I thought.

"I love Elvis Presley!" I squealed. "But I never read about him before. I didn't know half that much about him."

"That was the point," Rupert smiled, enjoying my excitement.

"I wonder what fried banana sandwiches taste like?" I asked, referring to what the book said was Elvis's favorite snack.

"I really can't imagine," Rupert laughed. "Now out of the way, child," he ordered. He told me to stand on the couch as he began pushing furniture back from the center of the room. He left only the coffee table in the middle. In the corner was his old record player. He retrieved an Elvis Presley album from a stack of records on the other side of the bookshelf and carefully placed it on the player. He pulled up chairs for each of us, close to the record player, and we listened.

"You will do some of your best learning in life by listening," he told me. And for nearly an hour we leaned toward the old record player, listening through the crackles and skips while Elvis crooned and rocked on.

"Listen to this part," Rupert would tell me repeatedly, pointing out all that he thought I could learn. "What about that high note?" he would ask me. I would nod and take it all in. "Great, great!" he would comment on a particular part. "Brilliant," he would say about another.

I was in heaven. I studied the side of Rupert's face as he listened and commented. I never met anyone before who seemed to enjoy and listen to and dissect music like I did. I wondered if this was what a soul mate was. When the record was over, he lifted the needle up from the player and told me to get up. He pulled the chairs away and pointed to the coffee table. "Up," he ordered again. Finally, I realized that he wanted me to stand on top of the coffee table. Hesitantly, I did. He disappeared for a moment into the kitchen, returning with a spatula. He handed it to me. "Your microphone, Mr. Presley," he said with a small nod. I stood dumbfounded. Certainly he didn't expect me to stand on the coffee table in the middle of the room and sing like Elvis Presley. But when he sat down at the old piano with his back to me and began to play "Love Me Tender," it became clear that that was exactly what he wanted me to do. I stood on the coffee table shaking my head back and forth.

"You can and you will," Rupert said. "Just try." I protested more, but Rupert William Holmes had a much stronger will than Noah Jacob had. And so I started singing, tentatively at first, but there was just something about Rupert—his strength, his encouragement, his total belief in me and the safety that came with all of that—that had me singing. And although I whispered and warbled my way through "Love Me Tender," by the time I got to "You Ain't Nothing But a Hound Dog" and "Jailhouse Rock," I was rocking that coffee table and wielding my spatula like a seasoned professional.

I don't think we ever laughed so hard. We were so loud that I don't know how many times it took for us to hear Edwin's voice yelling, "Hey kid, are you coming or not?" from the sidewalk. When we did hear him, we were both shocked and frozen for a second, then we dissolved into more laughter.

"You better get going, King," Rupert teased. I looked at the room in shambles. "I can take care of it." Rupert assured. "You better get going home."

I laughed and ran out of Rupert's door. "I'll see you tomorrow for school."

I called happily, "See you tomorrow."

And in essence, that was the School of Rupert Holmes, with seventy-eight-year-old Rupert Holmes III the teacher, and ten-year-old Noah Jacob the student, exploring and studying our loves of music and God together. And that was how we spent the rest of the summer. In the mornings we studied religion, every religion under the sun. All in all I bet we learned about almost thirty different religions, from the most obscure to the most common. Many I had heard of and many I had not. They were all in the big book, so we would read about them and talk about their similarities and differences. We would learn as much detail as we could from the black-and-white photos that accompanied the chapter.

"Learn from them all," Rupert would say. "You don't have to completely understand or agree with it, but you should learn from them all." Much of it was over my head, but I tried, learning that, if nothing else, I wanted to be a person with an open mind like Rupert.

On most days, I read about a different religion from the blue wool carpet in the living room. On Mondays, my favorite days, we found a church to visit, and I read from the big heavy book from alongside the highway on the way to the church All the while Rupert would correct my posture and enunciation, making me reread paragraphs until I got them right. Throughout the summer we visited six churches, all the churches in our town. I loved Mondays—"travelling days," Rupert would call them. "Field trips," I would call them. Rupert would put on his walking shoes and together we would go off into the world to find a church, to find God, and to remind Him that we were the Believers. It was amazingly fun to travel to the churches around the town, visiting them and exploring them firsthand.

In between, on our walks back and forth, we studied basic facts.

"The problem with new education," Rupert complained, "is that they got you kids learning such high-faluting stuff that they don't bother teaching you the basics. Well, that won't be a problem for you, Mr. Noah, you'll know the facts." And, boy, was he right! By the end of the summer, I knew more facts than I ever dreamed could be stuffed into my head. I knew states, capitals, spelling words, continents, oceans, math facts, history dates, presidents, the solar system, the constitution, the systems of the government, the systems of the body, famous artists, and any other list you could think of. By the end of the summer, I had it memorized.

Recess was always watching *The Price Is Right*, which I actually got quite good at playing and actually beat out Rupert for a couple of the showcases. "Beginner's luck," he would grumble with feigned anger, hiding the smile on his face.

After lunch, we did the same with the big book of music, studying great musical artists. The big book had every artist you could imagine from every genre and generation. We read about all of them, their beginnings, their big breaks, their careers, and where they were now or how they had died. Rupert had at least one record for every artist, and we would sit close to the old revolving turntable and listen and learn.

"Appreciate it all," Rupert would always say. "You don't have to love it or even like it, but appreciate it."

We read about them, listened to their music, and—on Mondays, because those days were special—I became them, standing on the coffee table with my spatula that had long stopped being a spatula and instead was a microphone.

Because of all the reading, listening, and studying, our days were filled with lively conversation, Rupert constantly asking me what I thought about this or that. I would try to dodge the question and ask him what he thought, but he would say that he already knew what he thought and that he wanted to learn something new too. After I told him my thoughts, I turned it around on him and told him that I wanted to learn something new. He would then play along. Never during any other season of my life would I learn more about anything, especially myself, than I did that summer. I look back and wonder what someone happening by and peeking through the front window of Rupert's house would have thought to see a tiny ten-year-old white boy and a gigantic seventy-eight-year-old black man reading, singing, dancing, and debating. They probably would not have realized that they were witnessing one of the most beautiful friendships God had ever created.

Signs

It was a stay-at-home day, a Wednesday, I think. We had been working in the backyard garden all morning long, pulling weeds. It was a stifling hot day. "Bet you wish you were at the pool today," Rupert said.

"Bet I don't," I replied with a grunt, pulling with both hands at a particularly stubborn weed.

Rupert tussled my hair. "You are a special one, Noah Jacob," he remarked. "You are a special one."

"Break time!" Rupert finally announced, leading us out of the garden. I flopped down in front of the pond while Rupert went off to get us drinks. He returned with two root beers and handed me one. We drank a bit, then lay back on the grass staring at the bright sunlight and beautiful blue sky that was dotted with puffy white, cotton-like clouds. It was a remarkably beautiful day. We lay there together, cooling off.

"Rupert?" I asked.

"Mmmm?" he answered. His eyes were closed. I could tell he was letting the breeze rush over him.

"Do you believe in signs?" I asked him.

"What kind of signs?"

"You know," I began struggling to put exactly what I meant into words, "like signs from up there," I motioned toward the sky. "From God, I guess—signs from God sent to us down here like messages."

Rupert was truly thinking on this one, I could tell. He turned and looked straight towards me. I had seen him look at me that way before like he was trying to figure something out about me. I realize now that he was weighing back and forth in his mind what he was going to say or if he was going to answer me at all. "You do test me," he finally said in an even tone with a sigh. "You do test me."

He turned, giving me his complete attention. "Yes, I do believe we get signs from above," he said. "But not half as often as people think. Some people run around claiming they see signs in just about everything, but I think what they really have," he said, "is faith—but they choose to see these things as signs." I nodded. "But nothing wrong with that either." Rupert insisted.

"How can we tell the difference between everyday faith and real signs from God?" I asked him. He thought for a moment. "It's just my opinion, of course, but I think a real sign from God comes with a certain kind of peace attached to it that doesn't go away."

This time I turned to face him. I know now that I was looking deeply into him. A small smile crossed his face, and he raised a playful eyebrow. "Have you had a sign, Noah Jacob?" he asked.

I shook my head slowly. "I think I'm too young."

"Then again, maybe you're not," he said, seriously.

"Have you had a sign, Rupert?" I asked.

"Yes. I believe I received a sign once," he answered straightly.

I lowered my head, not wanting to seem boastful that God had spoken directly to me. "I believe I have, just once too," I said shyly. This was going to take some courage on my part. I had never shared this with anyone.

"Tell me," Rupert encouraged.

"You first," I said.

Realizing I wasn't ready to share my story, he agreed. Rupert shifted, making himself comfortable on the grass and getting ready to tell his story. I turned over on my belly, propped my head on my hands, and got ready to listen. Rupert began, "It was about two months after my Ruby and Lilac left me," he began. "And well, I'm not sure how to put this, but I wasn't much at being a very nice person. The grief was eating me bit by bit, and I spent my days going to work and coming back home and not bothering with people and not bothering to be very nice to people who bothered with me.

"Now those were tough times for people," he went on to explain. "Lots of folks were having trouble making ends meet, so to make extra money people went door to door selling things—everything you could think of—light bulbs, brushes, vegetables, vacuums, you name it.

"It was a Saturday," he continued, "and as usual I was miserable, just sitting in my house. I had already gotten up three or four times to chase people away—not very nicely, I might add—to tell them that I wasn't buying, when the doorbell rang again. Well, madder than a hornet, I charged for the door, ready to make such a big fuss that word would get out and no one would ever have the courage to come knocking again." Like with all of Rupert's stories, I was caught with rapt attention. Now, I sat up straight.

"But when I opened the door, fully ready to fire like a cannon, I looked down to see a tiny, itty bit of a little girl half the size of you. She had a wagon bigger than she was, and she somehow had managed to lift it onto the porch. She looked exhausted, like she had been out all day long, which she probably had, but she forced herself to smile and said to me, 'Hi, mister. I'm selling these flower bulbs to help my family out, and I was wondering if you would like to buy one?'

"Now I was busy standing there like a balloon that just had all of the air taken out of it because the speech that I had planned on giving certainly couldn't be given to this tiny little girl. So I stood there with my mouth hanging open. Then finally I asked her, 'How much are they?'

"'One quarter' she said, hopeful. Then her face kind of dropped, and she said, 'The only problem is that I only have lilac left.'"

My eyes widened.

"Exactly," Rupert said. "I remember wincing when she said it, but I reached into my pocket and took out a quarter and handed it to her. She handed me the bulb which left her wagon empty. I lifted the wagon back down to the sidewalk for her and when I turned toward the house, she called back to me and said, 'Thanks, mister. My name is Ruby.'"

I stared now, not only wide-eyed but also dumbfounded. I had never heard such a story.

"So if I could humbly say," Rupert continued. "I do believe that my God spoke to me that day, telling me that not only were my Ruby and Lilac together, but they were fine too."

I was speechless except for one thought. "Did you plant it?" I asked him.

"That very day," he assured me.

"Did it grow?" I asked excitedly.

"Seems to have grown kind of nicely," he nodded with a grin on his face, motioning toward the lilacs that stretched from the front of the house around the side and clear to the back.

I laughed heartily. "All of that from one bulb?" I gushed. "Can't be!" I said, shaking my head wildly.

"Seems so," Rupert shrugged, laughing at both my reaction and the glory of it all. We were both quiet for a minute taking in the beauty.

"Now on to you, Mr. Noah," Rupert said. "Have you ever had a sign?"

I blushed, suddenly embarrassed. "Maybe," I said hesitantly.

"Yes or no," Rupert pressed, knowing it was yes. I nodded.

Rupert waited me out, letting his silence urge me on. I sighed, knowing that with Rupert, I would tell him just like I told him everything eventually. "It happened on my first day of school," I began. It was Rupert's turn to adjust himself and settle in. "I was terrified of going to school. Not a little bit," I emphasized. "A lot. It took both my mom and my dad to get me there."

"Why so scared?" Rupert asked.

"Just terrified of it all," I struggled to explain. "I was sure that I wouldn't have any friends and that everyone would hate me." He nodded.

"Now that summer, right before school started, something terrible happened. There was this boy named Chris Devon, and everyone loved him. He had just graduated from the elementary school, and he was always known for being the nicest kid in the school. He was everyone's friend, and he did it just by being himself. Every single year, from the year he started in first grade until the year he graduated, he got voted 'the nicest boy in the school.' But that summer, just a couple of weeks before school started, he was swimming at the community pool and he hit his head on the diving board and sunk to the bottom, and by the time people noticed and were able to get him up, he had already drowned."

Rupert shook his head back and forth. "Horrible sad," he mused. He nodded, encouraging me to go on to tell him what this had to do with me.

"Well, on the first day of school, after my mom and dad dragged me into the building, and the principal practically dragged me to the teacher, and the teacher put me in the seat, I just sat there and cried with my head down, not looking up at anything or anybody. And after a while, while I had my head down, through my tears I was able to see that etched in the pencil holder on the wooden part of the desk were the words 'Chris D was here.' It took me a minute to realize that it was his desk—the Chris D that everyone had been talking and crying about the last couple of weeks. I realized that when he first started school, he had sat in this very desk."

Now it was Rupert's turn for his eyes to widen and be glued to mine.

"And somehow," I said, struggling to find just the right words to explain how it made me feel, "somehow, it made me stop crying and made me less scared. I . . . I . . ." I was afraid to say the next part, but I did. "I somehow felt that he was there with me and, as little as I was, it made me somehow know that God was telling me what my purpose at school was supposed to be." Rupert nodded. "It made me think that maybe what God was telling me was to just be myself, be nice, and be everyone's friend, and carry on what Chris had started. I felt like God put me in his desk for a reason."

Rupert just kept nodding his head like he couldn't agree with me more. Little that I ever said made Rupert wide-eyed, but he was this time.

"So that's it," I said with a shrug.

"No, it's not," Rupert countered. "Who's been voted the nicest boy in the school every year since then?" He challenged.

I paused, a little embarrassed. I had planned on leaving that part out. "Me," I said meekly with my head down.

"Uh huh," Rupert said surely. "You bet you!" he said.

I looked up and smiled at him. He was being arrogant for me.

Then he said, lying on the grass, "I think you have been spoken to, Noah Jacob."

"And you too, Rupert Holmes," I told him.

"Sometimes, we Believers get lucky that way," Rupert said. I nodded.

We lay back on the grass with our eyes toward the sky, enjoying the quiet. As we lay there, way up high a jet silently went by, leaving a stream of white across the sky. Lazily we watched it disappear out of sight. Then, unexpectedly, it came back for a second pass, and the jet crossed from the other direction, leaving another stream of white, making a perfectly formed cross above us in the sky. We exchanged glances that needed no words of explanation and then broke into laughter. Rupert just shook his head back and forth as I lay giggling next to him.

The Holy Ghost

One Monday, we went to the Mormon church. I read out loud from the book to Rupert, and he nodded agreeably. The Mormon church was started by a farmer by the name of Joseph Smith. He had visions, one when he was fourteen telling him to start a church and another—a really neat one, if you ask me—when he was seventeen from an angel named Moroni who directed him to a book written on gold plates and buried in nearby hills. He dug them up, translated them, and they became *The Book of Mormon*. I told Rupert that in addition to the Bible, I was reading this as well. Secretly, I wanted to be like Joseph Smith and have an angel come and speak to me, but I kept this to myself. I was proud that I already knew almost all of what I read aloud to Rupert, but I did learn a few new things about my own faith, too. Rupert nodded, politely taking it all in.

"That sounds good to me," he would occasionally comment. "That makes perfect sense," he would say. I knew that he would be polite no matter what he thought, but I could tell he wasn't just trying to be polite. Rupert Holmes was probably the most open-minded person I would ever meet.

I read fast and chattered on excitedly. I was anxious and excited to show off the church that I loved. The Mormon church was tucked away about a mile and a half from Rupert's house. It was a long walk, but not the longest we would take that summer.

The thing that I liked the most about learning and talking to Rupert about religion was that it was different than doing it with anyone else. It was safer. He was completely nonjudgmental. With Rupert, I could really talk about religion and say anything and ask any question. With Rupert I could question things you weren't supposed to question. I could talk about how I was feeling even when I thought that I wasn't supposed to be feeling that way. Sometimes, it was difficult to do that in Sunday school.

Then I dared to ask him a question that had been worrying me, one that I would never have dared to ask in Sunday school. "Rupert," I began, still a little tentative, "do you believe in the Holy Ghost?"

Without hesitation, Rupert answered "You bet I do."

Feeling a little braver, I asked my real question. "Do you believe He talks to us?"

Again Rupert said without a pause, "I believe He talks and shouts and screams and sings and claps and whispers to us too." We walked a few paces in silence.

His answer troubled me. I guess my face and silence gave me away. "Tell me, child," he encouraged. I gulped. I swore I would never admit this to anyone in the whole world ever. But again, it was Rupert.

I sighed, imagining how relieved I might feel by saying it aloud weighed against how embarrassed I would be by saying it. I had a feeling Rupert already knew what I was going to say, so there really wasn't such a risk. I decided to just spit it out. "I don't think I can hear Him the way I'm supposed to," I said, letting out the air that I had been holding in my chest.

I waited for Rupert's response, which I expected to be quick and not exactly loud but animated still. Of course Rupert Holmes always surprised me. We walked in silence. I waited until he finally spoke. Instead of answering me though, he asked me questions. "When your mama hugs you, what do you feel?"

"Love," I answered surely.

"Why don't you knock old Edwin on his fanny every time he deserves it?" he asked.

"Because that would be wrong," I told him.

"Why do you pull my garbage to the curb for me instead of making my old bones do it?" he asked.

"Because it's the right thing to do," I told him.

"And who do you think is guiding you with all that?" Rupert asked, eyebrows raised. I smiled in spite of myself. Never in a million years would I have ever gotten to that conclusion so easily.

Rupert went on, "How many times did it take you to hear the G when we were singing Elvis?"

"A bunch," I admitted. I remembered that in a certain part of a song, I kept missing the G, and Rupert was relentless, making me listen to it again and again until I got it and nailed it on my own.

"Listen," Rupert said, tilting his head upward, calling my attention to a bird calling from a tree. "A whippoorwill," he told me. "Listen close." I did and memorized the sound. "Now hush and tell me when you hear it again," Rupert said. It didn't take long. There were chirps and calls from other birds in between, but after just about a minute a whippoorwill called again.

"There!" I said. Rupert smiled and nodded.

"It's all about practice," Rupert said simply. "Sometimes you hear the Holy Ghost without knowing it. Other times you just have to practice listening for Him." I smiled so big. He was right. Rupert was right again. I did hear the Holy Ghost. There was a spring in my step the entire way to the church.

When we got there, I was so excited to show Rupert everything that I was busting around like a fool. "Look, Rupert, look," I would say. "Isn't it beautiful? "Don't you think so?" I left him no time to answer.

"I do," he laughed, managing to get a word in.

"Aren't the bricks beautiful, and look at the steeple! Wait until you see the inside." I ran around, pulling on every door until I found an open one. I barreled through.

Rupert caught me in mid-fall. "Slow, child" he whispered. I needed that. Slowly we walked together down the center aisle.

"Isn't it beautiful." I whispered.

"Mighty, mighty beautiful," Rupert said surely.

Oh, how his answer pleased me! We found seats front and center and settled in. Rupert spoke first. "Noisy Noah's back," he said looking up to the altar. "And it isn't even a Sunday." I laughed out loud. "And he brought good old Rupert Holmes the third with him."

"We are Believers," I added.

"And we like what you believe here in this house," Rupert said. "And we came to say hello just in case you're Mormon." This part still kind of cracked me up, and I muffled a giggle.

"The part about getting into heaven by doing the good deeds," Rupert told God. "Now that is good stuff. And the selflessness and humbleness that you call for, well, the world would surely be better if we all followed that example. So what we're trying to say is, there's a lot of good preaching going on in here," he said. I sat next to Rupert, nodding my head emphatically. I couldn't have said it better myself. "And serving others," Rupert added. "We should all do more of that."

That seemed to just about cover it for us. We knelt and said our individual prayers shoulder to shoulder. After sitting a bit, Rupert thanked God for having us, and we walked slowly back down the center aisle, taking in the beauty and majesty of my church. Once outside, Rupert collected his pebbles from the steps and sidewalk around the church and we headed home.

We studied the solar system and the planets on the way home, with me carrying the big book most of the way. "The muscles in your arms are getting stronger, Mr. Noah," Rupert commented with a smile. I nodded, smiling back, hoping that he was right. I wolfed down lunch and fidgeted through the *Price Is Right*. I had peeked in the music book before we left, and it was Beatles' day and, boy, was I ready!

As always, at Rupert's insistence, we listened and studied first. I read from the big book about the history of the group. Then we sat together in the chairs around the old record player listening and studying technique, style, and lyrics. I took in every note and, when Rupert finally gave me permission, I nearly busted through the coffee table jumping on it with my spatula. For more than an hour, Rupert played, laughed, and encouraged while being my piano player, stage manager, and audience all at once. I of course, was John, Paul, George, and Ringo all at once too, I sang, drummed, guitar-ed and piano-ed my way through as I "Yesterday"-ed, "Hey Jude"-ed, "Let It Be," "Had a Ticket To Ride." and "Had a Hard Days Night" all afternoon long.

Sadly, three o'clock came, and Edwin stood on the sidewalk waiting for me.

"Goodbye, Rupert!" I called, stumbling out the door.

"Goodnight, Ringo," Rupert laughed after me. "Goodnight, Ringo."

Taking It With You

It was a Friday; we were out in the driveway washing Rupert's pride and joy, a cherry red 1950 Buick Le Sabre. It was a beautiful car in mint condition without a scratch on it. We washed it every Friday. "Got to get it ready for the weekend," he would joke. "Got to take my girl cruising on Saturday night." He winked at me.

Of course, we both knew he was kidding. The fact was, the car hadn't been moved in years, and he had absolutely no intention of driving again. He had let his license expire and carried no insurance on the car. But that didn't stop him from loving it. Rupert was not a materialistic man and lived very simply with few possessions, so the sight of the extravagant classic car in the driveway that was probably just a couple of inches shorter than the length of the entire house was quite a paradox. We washed the car just as gently as a mother washes a baby, and that was how Rupert liked it.

The first time, I only was allowed to watch from a safe distance away along the grassy patch that separated the gravel driveway and the walkway. As he washed, he described every move he made. He caressed more than washed, from the top to the bottom, and finished by polishing the wheels and hub caps. For the next couple of weeks, all I was allowed to wash were the wheels, then I moved up to scrubbing the hubcaps until I could see my face in them and my fingers were sore. Finally, with Rupert guiding me alongside him, I was allowed to wash the car with him. All the while, he guided and instructed me, saying, "Gentle now." "Not too hard." "A little more attention over here." "Not exactly seeing my face in that hubcap, Mr. Noah."

I worked hard and loved it. Together we washed and dried with the softest cloths that I had ever felt until it shone. Then with a sheepskin cloth, we polished the car until it sparkled. On sunny days the glare was nothing short of blinding. When we were done, Rupert popped the hood, and we would inspect the engine of the car. "The heart," Rupert would call it. It was almost as clean as the outside of the car.

Then finally came my favorite part when Rupert would announce, "Let's start the old girl up!" I always got butterflies in my stomach when he said this. The inside of the car was spotless too, of course, with white leather seats that still smelled like new and looked like they had never been sat upon and knobs so shiny they looked like they had never been touched. I would carefully climb into the passenger seat as Rupert eased himself into the driver's seat. For my benefit, he would always make it quite dramatic, placing the key in the ignition, looking sideways at me, raising his eyebrows in anticipation, and then with a turn of the key, he would start the car. "Purrs like a kitten!!" he would announce each time, shaking his head back and forth with satisfaction. I would laugh at his excitement every time. I loved seeing him happy. We would let it run for exactly ten minutes. Rupert would time it on his wristwatch. I would smile at Rupert as he adjusted the mirrors around him and then, with both hands on the wheel, he would melt into the seat. I always felt honored to be sitting next to him.

Some Fridays, I would just end up laughing the entire ten minutes because Rupert would joke, "Unfortunately, the radio is broken but fortunately for you, I know how to sing," and he would then belt out show tunes for ten solid minutes as I laughed hysterically and begged him to stop. Other times we would talk. We had some of our best conversations of the summer inside that car in those ten minutes.

"Who says you can't take it with you?" Rupert scoffed one particular Friday.

"Everyone!" I answered without thinking. He looked at me with raised eyebrows. My answer was quick and bordering on disrespectful. "Well," I squeaked with my voice a little nervously high. "that is what everyone says."

"Well, everyone is wrong," he growled as he looked around himself at his pride and joy and smiled. "I'll be taking this girl with me." He laughed.

"Maybe you will," I said, getting in the spirit of the idea. "Maybe when you get to heaven, it will be one of the things waiting for you. Maybe everyone gets just one thing that they are allowed to take with them," I said.

"Now you're talking," Rupert complimented. "All I know is this baby is coming with me." Rupert ran his fingers around the steering wheel and then used the sleeve of his shirt to dust off the radio knobs. He said. "What one thing will you take with you?"

Without a thought I replied, "My dog." He nodded.

I loved my dog, Marshmallow. My mother insisted that I be the one to name him because I was the only one among my siblings who wasn't fighting on the way home when we went to pick him up. Everyone always gave me a hard time about his name, but that's what he felt like to me when I hugged him. And now three years later he slept only on my bed and came to me when he needed to be walked or wanted food or water. I definitely would take him along to heaven with me.

We relaxed in the car for a few minutes with Rupert belting out a couple of unwanted show tunes and with me protesting, when all of a sudden he jerked up straight in his seat and said, "Oh, no!" as he looked out the window. He checked the time on his watch. We were at nine minutes and forty-nine seconds. We began our traditional countdown, but he seemed nervous, looking from the watch to the street at something that at first I couldn't make out. We counted down, "10, 9, 8." We counted "7, 6, 5" and continued "4, 3, 2, 1." Instantly Rupert clicked off the car. "Out," he ordered, almost like he was scared. He jumped out and so did I. I had no idea what was happening, but something had him spooked.

Once out on the sidewalk, I could see an elderly lady ambling towards us from across the street. Rupert eyed her with trepidation. "Oh, jeez," he muttered. I stared at him. He actually looked a little scared. "Every Friday," he muttered. She was old and slow. We had time to talk as we waited for her. "Woman has been trying to get a ride in my car for forty years," he grumbled. "Well, it isn't happening, no matter how sweet she comes on to me." I was bug-eyed. I couldn't believe my ears. "Watches me wash it every Friday, then brings me a casserole to try and sweet talk me into a Saturday night drive." I was trying not to laugh.

"You're kidding me," was all I could say.

"First thing you do when you're sixteen," he told me, "is get a cool car. Attracts women like bees to honey."

"A chick magnet," I said.

"Whatever," he answered. She had almost reached us.

"Hello, Mr. Rupert," the old woman greeted. She had silvery-blue hair and looked like my grandmother.

"Miss Margaret," Rupert greeted back with a nod.

"Couldn't help but see you polishing that beautiful car of yours and thought you might be working on an appetite," she said, handing Rupert a casserole dish.

"How mighty nice of you," Rupert acknowledged, taking the dish. "I sure did enjoy last Friday's."

I was almost embarrassed to be there and was grateful that for the moment I seemed to be invisible to them. But it only lasted a moment.

"And who might this be?" she asked, eyeing me up. Rupert looked down at me and I looked up at him. I had no idea how he would answer. "Why this here is my grandson, Noah," he said. His words were music to my ears. To say that the woman looked shocked would be an understatement.

"Why, Mr. Rupert," she said, almost gasping. "I never knew."

"Me either," Rupert agreed. "Just showed up one day." This made the old woman's eye almost bulge clear out of her head.

"I keep leaving him in the sun, but nothing seems to help," Rupert said, acting dismayed. I was trying so hard not to laugh. The poor woman had no idea what to do with all of this. The confused look stayed on her face until I think it all became too much for her and she turned to leave. Rupert thanked her again for the casserole, and she left, looking slightly annoyed. We watched as she ambled back across the street.

"Rupert!" I hissed when she was out of earshot. "I think you made her mad."

"I hope not," he said dismissively, giving the dish a sniff. "Oh good! Tuna. The woman does make a mean Friday casserole." I slugged him in the arm. "What was that for?" he laughed.

"You told her you leave me in the sun!" I squealed.

"Yeah, that was a good one," he laughed, pleased with himself.

We spotted Edwin and his friend coming down the street, so we sat down on the porch steps to wait.

"And you called me your grandson," I pointed out a little softly, a little bashfully, and a whole lot proud.

"Stuck for words," Rupert said.

"You're never stuck for words," I pointed out quietly. "You never say what you don't mean." There was a pause. I studied his face as he studied the sky.

"Maybe not," he finally answered. It was the one and only time I ever saw Rupert's face flushed with color. He fiddled with his fingers.

"Maybe you meant it," I said.

"Maybe," he answered, just barely loud enough for me to hear and with a tiny smile on his face. My smile, on the other hand, was so big that my face hurt.

I jumped off the steps and joined Edwin and his friend on the sidewalk. I couldn't remember ever being happier. From the sidewalk I called nice and loud. "Bye, Grandpap! See you on Monday!" Rupert looked up and smiled a huge grin that matched mine, and he shook his head back and forth.

That night I had a dream about Rupert and me up in heaven driving in his cherry red Le Sabre, with him behind the wheel, me in the passenger seat, and Marshmallow in the back seat, the two of us laughing like crazy as we serpentined through puffy white clouds.

Making It Snow

We were on our way to the Jewish synagogue. It was about a mile and a half from Rupert's. The walks no longer seemed long, no matter how far away the church. We were both used to our walks by now and, when we had lively conversation like we did on that day, they flew by.

"So when you get to heaven," I asked him, "what's the first thing you'll say to God?"

He laughed and shrugged, "Probably just thanks for having me,"

I smiled. "Great answer."

"And you?" he asked.

"Probably just 'I'm home,' like I do now."

He smiled a genuine smile at me. "Great answer yourself," he said.

"What's the first thing you'll ask Him to do?" I continued.

"Don't think I ever thought of that," Rupert admitted. "I guess to see my wife and baby." Of course that made sense. I checked his face to see if I had made him sad, and it seemed somehow that I had done the opposite. I could tell by reading the expression on his face that he was letting himself visualize the meeting. I stayed quiet, not wanting to interrupt.

After a few minutes he asked me, "What's the first thing you'll do?" I was glad that he asked because I was so anxious to answer.

"There are so many things," I gushed excitedly, "but I know that I'd sign up for the choir right away." This made him laugh and shake his head.

"What?" I asked him, stopping in the middle of the sidewalk.

"Noah Jacob, you do please me," he said, tousling my hair. "You do please me."

I went on, "Then I would ask if I could make it snow and hail."

"Both?" Rupert asked with a raised eyebrow.

"Definitely both," I told him. "I definitely want to make it snow and hail, especially if it's July."

Rupert laughed and laughed. "Don't be surprised if He says 'no,'" he warned.

"Why would He?" I asked indignantly. "It's my heaven."

"It's His heaven first," Rupert reminded me. He was right.

"I think you might be the first person to ever be sent back down for being a pain in the neck," he chuckled. "Poor God just might decide that you're too much work, and He might not be ready for you."

This time I laughed. "I hope so," I told him.

"Why in the world would you want that?" Rupert asked.

"Imagine how popular I would be when I got back down here." Rupert shook his head. "I mean, I would be the first guy ever who had gone up there, seen what it's like, then come back down and tell everyone about it."

"I changed my mind," Rupert said. "Think He'll probably just keep your pain in the neck self up there." I pushed him playfully on the arm. We walked a bit longer in silence with thoughts of heaven swimming in and out of my head.

"Do you think we'll sleep on clouds?" I asked him.

"We just might," Rupert acknowledged.

I was quiet for a moment, then I said, "I hope our clouds are close to one another."

After a few paces, Rupert replied, placing a hand on top of my head. "I'm sure they will be, child. I'm sure they will be."

Rupert was right about one thing. My arms were definitely getting stronger, because I could easily balance the book while walking and reading about the Jews and their faith. I knew almost nothing and Rupert admitted that neither did he but, we both found it strange that we had always viewed Judaism as being so different than Christianity. In lots of ways it was, but there were also so many similarities between the two faiths. When we got to the synagogue, we examined the outside of the modern-looking building. The unique symbol caught my attention. We knew from our reading that it was called the Star of David or the Shield of David, and it was named after King David of ancient Israel. It was a unique hexagram shape. I thought it interesting.

Stepping into the darkened synagogue, we noticed the basket containing the yarmulkes. We each took one and placed them on our heads. We noted the simplicity of the inside. No pews, cushioned chairs instead. Even after our reading, we still weren't sure of many of the Jewish customs, so we just sat quietly for awhile, praying silently, shoulder to shoulder, hoping the prayers we knew worked in this house. Then Rupert introduced us as the Believers and once again explained how we were in the area and thought it would be all right for us to stop by and check in, just in case He was Jewish. I did tell him I thought Hanukkah seemed neat and menorahs were really pretty. After another spell of sitting quietly, Rupert thanked Him for having us, and we excused ourselves.

"That was nice," we both agreed on the way out. Rupert collected his pebbles and stones along the outside of building, and we headed home. That day on the way back to Rupert's house, we studied about world leaders. I kept stumbling over how to spell Mahatma Gandhi. But after fifty times of Rupert making me do it over and over, I got it right.

Once at home, we had cheese sandwiches and root beers for lunch and *The Price Is Right* for recess. There was no gloating from either one of us that day; we both lost our showcases. Rupert commented on Bob Barker's fine head of hair. "When you go grey," he told me, "go grey. No hair dye." I promised.

He went to get my spatula from the kitchen while I pushed back all of the furniture. I had been begging all morning for him to tell me who we would be learning about that day, but he refused to even give me a hint. I went to retrieve the big book from the shelf, but Rupert caught me and slapped my hand away. He held the book closed for a few moments that seemed like hours, then dramatically opened it.

"Oh, yeah!" I squealed, when I saw who it was. "Frank Sinatra!" I announced.

"Ol' Blue Eyes!" Rupert shouted.

"Wait, let's see," he said, taking my chin and looking deep into my eyes. "Uh," he said feigning mock disappointment. "More hazel," he grumbled. "But I guess they'll do."

As always, I stood in the middle of the woven rug and read aloud the biography. This time we already knew much. Joking, we decided that we were a two-man Rat Pack and would have been great members of the real one. Then we listened as Frank Sinatra sang to us from the old record player, Rupert having to push the needle past the cracks and scratches. Then, atop the coffee table, I became him. I was Frank Sinatra with a spatula and hazel eyes. When Rupert thought I wasn't giving it my all, he called me "Ol' Hazel Eyes," but when I sang with my whole heart, he called, "Thatta boy, Blue Eyes," over his shoulder as he played the piano. I "New York"-ed, "New York"-ed, let "Luck Be a Lady," all by doing it "My Way."

At three o'clock, which came much too soon, I headed out. I called, "Bye, Rupert," knowing that he was going to call me anything but Noah.

I was right, of course. As I hopped down the steps of the porch to the sidewalk, he called, "See you, ol' Hazel Eyes."

Then, grumbling loudly, he said, "Only was and only is ever going to be one ol' Blue Eyes." Then I heard him chuckle to himself.

Hazel was close enough to blue for me. I was just glad to be a part of the Rat Pack.

Good and Bad

"Darn kids," Rupert muttered. "If I ever find you doing such nonsense, I'll give you a whipping you'll never forget," he promised, fishing in the tool box for just the right nails while holding one in his mouth. We were repairing and painting the fence along the sidewalk in front of Rupert's house. The night before some rowdy teenagers went joy riding through the neighborhood, knocking down mailboxes and fences and tossing out empty beer cans along the way.

"I won't," I promised.

"Better not," he threatened again. "But there's going to be temptation, you know?" He pounded in one of the nails.

"I know," I said.

"And sometimes, it's not going to be easy to stay away from," he reminded me.

"I know," I said again, wishing that he would give me more credit. I wasn't sure if Rupert realized it or not, but a kid my age had usually already faced much more temptation than he thought. I was a good kid who stayed away from trouble fairly easily, but that didn't mean that trouble wasn't all around me. I probably would have found trouble at the pool, too, if I had been going with Edwin.

"Rupert," I asked him, "what's the worst thing you've ever done?"

"Too bad for you to know," Rupert assured me.

"Come on, Rupert," I pleaded. "I can take it."

"Nope," he said firmly and continued painting the fence as if I wasn't there. I walked away sulking. I was mad. I continued to pick up the beer cans in Rupert's yard.

"Get the ones from the neighbors' yards, too," he told me. "Do for others."

After finally tossing them all in a bag, I plopped down about fifteen feet behind him as a kind of silent protest. He glanced back and saw me.

"Don't be pouting at my back," he warned. I continued my strike.

"Come over here," he said, still continuing to paint, but his voice serious now.

"Don't make me repeat myself," he said without turning around. I knew I didn't want to do that. I stood up and walked the few feet and sat down beside him. He pulled me in front of him and put the paint brush in my hand. With his hand over top of mine, he guided our hands together up and down.

"Not because you pouted," he said sternly. I nodded.

"I hurt someone who did not do one thing to me," he began as we painted together. "I was young and stupid, about fourteen, and I wanted to fit in. I was getting ready to join a group of pretty rough boys, a gang you might call it. I had just started hanging around with them, and in my stupid head that seemed like a privilege. Well, they told me if I wanted to stay with them, then I needed to do this initiation. They told me I had to pick a fight with someone who never did one blessed thing to me. It was a Saturday night, and we had planted ourselves on a corner. They said they would pick the guy and, in front of them, I would have to beat him up." I was trying so hard not to react. I could never imagine my gentle Rupert doing such a thing.

"Well, after a while along comes this poor soul who would never hurt a fly and they picked him. I was scared out of my mind and sick to my stomach and afraid to do such a horrible thing, and afraid not to do it with them standing there watching me. Well, I was a coward," he said pulling his hand away and letting me paint on my own. He had taken a seat on the grass behind me. "So the coward that I was," he continued, "I did it. I beat up this poor defenseless guy and left him bruised and bloody on the sidewalk and ran away with them, laughing and congratulating me as being officially one of them."

I was too stunned to speak. Rupert took the brush back, and we switched places. He began touching up the spots I had missed. "What happened?" I asked him.

"I got away from them as soon as I could," he said. "I ran away from them and went and threw up in an alley. I never once associated with one of them again. I went home and decided, then and there, I would never be that person. I got down on my knees at the edge of my bed and promised God that if He would only forgive me, then I would never use my hands for anything but good for the rest of my life." I nodded. Rupert never stopped amazing me and being my hero.

"And I kept that promise, and I am proud of that, but to this day I am ashamed of what I did. That part will never go away."

"God forgave you, Rupert," I told him.

"I think so, too," he said.

"Did you ever see that guy again?" I asked.

"Now and again," Rupert said.

"Did you ever say anything to him?" I asked.

"Another shame," Rupert sighed. "I never had the courage to apologize to him." I felt bad for Rupert.

He closed the paint container, tapping it shut with the handle of the screw driver. As we put the tools and paint supplies in the garage, Rupert asked, "And you, Mr. Noah, what's the worst thing you ever did?" My stomach squeezed. And all of a sudden I could understand Rupert's hesitation to tell me his story, because now I felt so embarrassed to tell him mine. I sighed, knowing that I might as well get it over with because I always eventually told him everything.

"It's actually a little like yours," I began. "I was kind of forced into it too. I was about seven and on vacation with my family and our cousins and, since they were all older, we were allowed to go out and walk the boardwalk with them. Me and my other cousin were the youngest and just real happy to be along with them until we found out what they had planned. They made us all go into this drugstore. They were trying to buy cigarettes, and they told us exactly what to do because they had it all planned out. My oldest cousin, who was about sixteen, went in and asked to buy the cigarettes, knowing that the man behind the counter would tell him that he was too young, so my cousin acted all innocent and said he was sorry and that they were for his dad and that he would go out and get him. So the man, thinking that this was true, left them lying on the counter. Then they told my other cousin who was as young as me to knock something over in another part of the store so that the manager would go running and they would be able to grab the cigarettes and run out. They said if we didn't follow their plan, they would be mean to us for the entire vacation, and we were afraid of them. So we did exactly what they said, and it worked exactly like they planned." I put my head down. I was still so ashamed. I waited to hear what Rupert would say.

"The devil's temptation comes in all forms," he finally murmured thoughtfully. "Did you ask for forgiveness?"

"Like crazy," I told him.

He answered my question before I could ask him what. "He forgave you as soon as you were sorry, Noah." I nodded, wanting this to be true.

"I disliked my cousin every single day since then," I admitted.

"Rightfully so," Rupert acknowledged. "But let that go, too. Bad feelings consume a good heart, and I suspect he's not even worth hating." I nodded in agreement. I had heard hushed conversations between my mother and father since then about how that cousin had been into a lot of trouble since then.

"Once or twice in a life," Rupert said, "you step away from yourself to remind yourself who you really are," I nodded. This was a lot for a ten year old to understand, but I was pretty sure that I knew what he meant. I was just happy that Rupert was sure that God had forgiven both of us.

We were carrying the supplies back to the shed. "What's the best thing you've ever done?" I asked him. This was a much happier question.

"Well, I'm not quite sure that I can answer that," Rupert said.

"Yes, you can," I told him. "You're just being too modest." He laughed.

"At least tell me one thing," I said. I could tell he was thinking as he placed the supplies back on the shed shelf as I handed them to him. I watched as his face grew a bit sad-looking. I could tell he found something. He looked at me, and he knew with my eyes glued to him the way they were that there was no way out.

He looked at me with a serious look like he always did when he was about to tell me something that he didn't want to. "No interruptions or questions," he said firmly.

I nodded in agreement. "I promise."

"Before Ruby and I got married, I was in the army. I had a good friend. He died. Right before he died, he wrote a letter to his mother. After I travelled back to the States, I travelled on eight busses for four days to put it in her hands," he said with a shrug. "So maybe that."

"Definitely that," I told him. I watched as Rupert raised his head and stared off into the sky for a minute, taking himself to another time and another place. I thought it strange how the most telling stories need the fewest words. I had no questions because I understood completely. Rupert Holmes III, like I had been suspecting all summer long, was a genuine hero. As we walked back to the house, I said, "I bet his mom thanks God for you every night in her prayers."

Rupert stopped walking, looked down at me like he was seeing me for the first time, then just sighed and shook his head back and forth. He started walking again with his hand on top of my head and didn't move it until I climbed up onto the porch swing. Rupert lowered himself lazily into his rocking chair. "Well, I told you. Now it's your turn. What's the best thing you ever did?" I had been waiting for him to ask, so I was ready.

"It's not as good as yours," I began.

"I'll be the judge," Rupert noted.

"I was in the first grade," I began, "and this boy, Timothy Goodman, kept raising his hand because he had to go to the bathroom. Well, it was silent time and that was against the rule so the teacher kept ignoring him and finally he just wet his pants. And it was awful for him. The teacher got mad, and the whole class laughed. So when we were out at recess, he was still so sad, sitting all by himself on a curb wearing some leftover, too small clothes that the school nurse made him put on. Well, the other kids, thanks to the meanest kid in the class, noticed him sitting there and started dancing around him taking turns tapping him on the head, calling him Pee Boy. Well, he just sat there and when he didn't move or defend himself at all, it ended up being practically everybody in the whole school yard teasing this one kid. Everybody was taking their turn until every single one of them had done it. Well, the real mean kid noticed that I hadn't joined in and kept telling me to go over and do it too. He even made two of his friends try to drag me over to do it. But instead, I just went over and sat down next to Timothy and told him that it would be OK."

Rupert nodded his approval. "And what happened?" he asked.

"Well," I grimaced, "they ended up dancing around me and tapping me on the head and calling me Pee Boy Junior." Now Rupert grimaced.

"I was kind of hoping for a better outcome," he said chuckling.

"Me too," I said laughing with him.

"Well," Rupert said, sinking a little more deeply into the chair, "it looks like we both have some miles on us, Noah Jacob."

"I guess so," I yawned, now lying back on the swing. Rupert rocked easily back and forth, and I let my mind drift as I wondered whether I would be anyone's hero someday. Together we enjoyed the comfortable silence of our friendship, letting our minds fill with calming thoughts. Rupert had long been asleep when Edwin approached a half hour later. I tiptoed off the porch whispering, "See you tomorrow, Rupert." I smiled as he shifted peacefully in the rocker and began to snore.

Down There

We were on our way to the Baptist church, which would have been Rupert's church if he still went to church regularly. But he said that since Ruby and Lilac died, he preferred to do his praying at home. As we walked, I read about Baptists out of the heavy book. I could not tell if Rupert already knew about all that I was reading or not, because he just kept nodding and saying "uh huh" in the same way. But I was sure learning something. "Baptists seem, seem kind of . . ." I was stuck for a word that Rupert plugged in for me.

"Animated," Rupert finished with a laugh. "Let's just say animated, or maybe passionate."

"Fire and brimstone," I commented.

"You betcha," was Rupert's response.

"Rupert?" I asked him "Do believe there really is a . . . a . . ."

"You can say it," Rupert said, giving me permission to say it, but I still couldn't.

"A 'down there,'" I said instead. Rupert pondered. More than any adult in my life, he took my questions seriously and really answered them.

"Tough question," he admitted, "but I do believe there is." This was a sad answer, a difficult concept for me to imagine. I almost flinched as I let loose the images that I had stored in my head.

"But if God is always good and always forgiving, then why doesn't He let all people into heaven?" I asked.

"So you do use that head of yours for more than just growing hair," he smiled. "Let's put it this way, Mr. Noah," Rupert said. "What you said is the same argument that all believers use, and it sure is a good one." I brightened up. If a zillion other believers asked the question before me, there must be an answer. Rupert dashed that hope. "Just not an answerable question is all," Rupert said flatly.

"Why not?" I asked, a little mad.

"Because no one ever has come back to tell us," Rupert laughed.

"Aw, Rupert," I whined, giving him a playful punch in the arm.

"Well, don't get mad at me," he laughed. "It sure isn't my fault."

"I don't want there to be a 'down there,'" I confessed seriously. "I want it to work out for everyone."

"It just may," Rupert offered.

"But how?" I reasoned, "If there is a 'down there,' then there must be someone in it"

"Maybe not," Rupert offered again. "Maybe God just takes you to the door and lets you have a good long peek inside until you get real good and sorry and—"

I became excited and cut him off, "And once you're good and sorry, He forgives you and you don't have to go in."

"Bingo!" Rupert called and laughed. I laughed, too. We walked the rest of the way to the Baptist church in silence. I liked Rupert's theory and played it out in my head several times, imagining sinners at the gates of "down there," repenting and being forgiven.

When we got to the church, Rupert didn't talk much. We just entered the simple building quietly and found our seats. It was less ornate than the other churches we had visited but no less beautiful. I realized for the first time that there was a lot of beauty in simplicity. Rupert seemed to settle in the seat a little more, but somehow at the same time seemed to be a little more uncomfortable. I didn't say anything because I didn't want to rush him. He almost seemed as if he had business to take care of. And knowing him like I did, I was right. After a few minutes he began. "Well," he paused and cleared his throat, "it isn't that I stopped praying. but of course you know that. I just do my praying different since then." He was talking to God directly from the deepest part of his heart, and I was honored to be there witnessing it. I sat still in the pew next to him. I almost felt like I shouldn't be there, but I was glad that I was.

"I guess all I'm trying to say is that I'm still a Believer, and I'm still thankful for the life you've given me, and I would be mighty, mighty grateful if someday, when you see fit, you would let me see my Ruby and my Lilac again. Amen," he concluded.

"Amen," I whispered.

He leaned back in the pew and settled in. He was done. I wondered just how many years he had waited to come back to this church and say those words. After a couple of minutes I reached out and, in the only way a ten year old would know how to console a friend, I put my hand on his back. "He will, Rupert," I whispered softly. "He'll let you see them again. I'm sure of it." Rupert turned to me and nodded and gave me a small, startled smile. I think for a few minutes he may have forgotten that I was there. He reached over to me and put a hand on the top of my head.

"This here, God, is Noah," he said, introducing me and turning back into his old self. "He is a Believer like me. We're Believers." I smiled at him. "And we were in the neighborhood," he said with a wink to me, "and we thought we'd stop by just in case you were a Baptist." He paused for a moment and then said, "Keep up the good work." I almost laughed. Rupert seemed to have run out of things to say so I took over.

"And even though people don't exactly like it," I said, anxious to tell God what I thought, "I think the fire and brimstone stuff is good for people. At school we always learn more from the teachers who we're scared to death of." I looked over and Rupert, of course, was laughing a hearty, silent laugh at my words. I nudged him to stop.

"I agree," he said, with just a little bit of teasing in his voice. I didn't care. I had been practicing what I was going to say for the entire mile-long walk.

"And the singing and clapping, I like that, too," I said. "Church shouldn't always have to be stuffy."

I was done talking and so it seemed was Rupert. For a few more minutes we sat in a peaceful, satisfied silence. Then Rupert thanked God for His time and excused us, and we walked out of one the most beautifully simple places I had ever been. After he picked a few pebbles and stones from the sidewalk, we headed home. On the way we studied the states, capitals, and presidents. I swear I had to spell "Eisenhower" fifty times before I spelled it right. Our cheese sandwiches and root beers were as good as always. *The Price Is Right* was as fun as always. Rupert had a little extra skip in step on his way to get to the big music book, because he slaughtered me on the showcase and won by about $20,000 because I misjudged how much a trip to Aruba and a moped would cost. When he opened the music book, my face dropped.

"Now wait a minute!" I protested instantly. "I don't think I want to do this."

"You will," Rupert laughed.

"No, Rupert," I whined, knowing he could make me do anything he wanted me to do.

"I don't want to be a girl," I protested. Rupert laughed heartily again.

"Not just any girl," he said, acting insulted. "Judy Garland!" He bellowed.

"I know she was great and all," I admitted, "but she was still a girl."

"Nobody's saying she wasn't," Rupert said as he pushed back the furniture, cleared the coffee table, and got my spatula. "The point is, she was great." He pushed me to the center of the woven carpet and handed me the book. "Read," he ordered. Of course I obeyed and read about Judy Garland's life and times. The reading made me pensive.

"It seems so strange that someone could have so much and be so unhappy," I said.

"Not so strange," Rupert insisted. "The same way that people can have so little and be so happy," he reminded. I nodded he was right. After just a little more protesting on my part, we went ahead and listened to Judy Garland's amazingness as the record crackled and her voice trickled beautifully through the old record player. Then, before I knew it, I was on the coffee table and singing Judy Garland—in a manly way, of course. Rupert called me Joe to help me save face and hollered and encouraged, "Sing it, Joe!" He plunked on his piano keys until it was 3:00 and Edwin had appeared.

"Night, Rupert!" I called on my way out the screen door.

"Good night, Judy!" he yelled with an extra loud belly laugh. I tried, but couldn't keep myself from laughing with him. Actually, I laughed most of the way home while Edwin and his friend looked at me like I was crazy, which only made it all the more funny.

A Rainy Day

It was a rainy Tuesday at Rupert's house. I got away with leaving the house by telling my mom that the pool manager let Edwin and me clean up and do odd jobs around the pool on rainy days in exchange for extra snacks. I felt guilty because this pleased her. But I wasn't about to skip a day of seeing Rupert. The rain would trickle down the window steadily, then every once in awhile it would gush, and thunder would crash and lightning would light up the entire house. We were playing gin, one of the many card games Rupert would teach me that summer. I jumped when the thunder boomed.

"Nothing to be afraid, of child," Rupert soothed. I nodded. We kept playing.

I wondered what the people in heaven were doing right then. Was it raining in heaven? Were the folks up there making it rain down here by pushing down buckets of water on top of us? Were they laughing and enjoying doing it? What about the thunder? When I was very little, they told me that the angels were bowling and that the really loud claps were strikes, but I was too old for that, even if I didn't exactly have an explanation for the thunder. I was pretty sure that the lightning was just a great big light switch being turned on. The lightning flashed and the thunder crashed again. I winced. I couldn't concentrate on the game. Rupert, knowing this, said, "Let's finish this game later." He got up and pulled his rocker over to the window. I stood my ground in the middle of the room.

"Sometimes if you look at what scares you long enough," he said, lighting up his pipe and settling into his chair, "it takes the fear out of it." I was hesitant to move closer, but I did. I went over to the window, fearfully anticipating the next crash, and cautiously looked out. And when it did crash, I jumped a mile, heading back to the center of the room. Rupert reached with just one arm and stopped me, pulling me close to him, then onto his lap. I breathed deeply. "Just rain," he insisted softly. From the safety of his lap I felt better, the lightning seemed less intense and the thunder just a touch quieter. My breathing became normal, and we sat in silence just taking it in. Maybe Rupert was right; maybe all I needed to do was to watch it awhile.

My mind began to wander again back to the people in heaven. "Rupert?" I asked him.

"Mmmmm?" He replied taking a long drag from his pipe.

"Can I ask you something?"

"Uh huh," he said.

"Are you afraid of dying?" I wasn't sure if this was an OK question to ask or not. I figured that it wasn't one that you asked most people, but Rupert wasn't most people, so maybe it was an OK question for him. The way that he gently blew the smoke out in perfect rings before he answered told me that it was OK. I playfully swatted at them with my fingers, waiting for him to answer.

"No, I believe I am not," he answered.

"Really?" I questioned, turning just a bit to look at his face. "Not even a little?"

He nodded surely. We rocked back and forth in silence a few times before he said, "And you?"

I nodded. "A little," I admitted.

"And the reason?" he asked.

"Cause I won't know anybody," I told him.

He smiled after I said this and chuckled just a bit. "That actually makes sense," he told me. "Not sense that I would have thought of, but good sense. You see the difference with me is that I'll know everybody," he laughed. "When you get to be my age, you find that you know more people up there than you know down here." I nodded. This was something of which I would never have thought.

We rocked silently for several minutes until a thought made my heart leap with fear. "Rupert!" I yelped suddenly, turning fully to face him. Rupert's saying that he knew more people up there than down here had just sunk in. "You don't want to die now, do you?"

He smiled gently. "No, child," he assured me. "I'm more than willing to wait my turn." I sighed hard and fell back onto him, relieved.

"What do you think it feels like?" I asked him.

After another puff, he said with certainty, "Just going to sleep."

"Even if—." He cut me off.

"No matter how," he insisted. "Just like going to sleep. No matter what it looks like or how it happens down here. It's all the same." I was glad he was so sure of this, because I wanted to think of it this way. "And when it is your time," he continued, "you'll know plenty of folks when you get there."

After a moment, Rupert added, "And you'll know Him, and that's all that will matter." He motioned toward his Bible that sat on the coffee table next to the sofa. "That is if you're keeping up with your reading," he said with a raised eyebrow. Rupert was always after me to read my Bible every day and, since meeting him, I wasn't doing too badly with my promise. I knew that he read his every day because many days as I was walking out the door at three o'clock, I would see him pick it up and settle onto the sofa.

"I'll know Him when I get there," I told him. "I hope we go together." I told him.

"Don't wish for that," he insisted. "It would be the wrong order of things. I will go first and, after you've finished down here, you come find me." I nodded. I guessed he was right. We watched the drops of rain fall in individual water droplets that somehow found each other and huddled together in bigger, stronger pools on the window panes.

"Do you think there are pearly gates?" I wondered.

"Imagine so," Rupert answered.

"So if I get there first," I asked him, "you don't want me to wait, you want me to go right in?"

"Of course," he insisted. "Go ahead in and get things set up, and I'll meet you there. But that's not going to happen.... I'm going to go first."

Before I could start protesting again, he said, "It's not sad. It's just the order."

"You do the same," I told him with a nod. "Don't wait. Get set up."

"Will do," he promised. We rocked back and forth.

"I hope there won't be questions," I lamented. I confused him with this one.

"What kind of questions?" he asked.

"You know, to get in," I answered. "I hope there are not real hard questions that you have to answer to get by the pearly gates."

"Oh, there will be," Rupert assured me. "But just one." He knew that this would get me riled up.

"Tell me," I insisted.

He shook his head, "No."

"Please," I begged.

Another "No."

"Pleeeeeeeeease," I whined.

He threw his head back and laughed, "The only question He's going to ask you is 'Did you do your best?'" I nodded in relief. "Are you going to be able to answer 'Yes' to that one?"

"I am," I said firmly. Rupert nodded.

Both satisfied, we rocked back and forth as we watched the rain—the rain that wasn't so scary anymore.

God's Smile

We were on our way to the Presbyterian church. I read from the book as I walked. We found out that the Presbyterian church was first formed with a merger between English and Scottish people. Actually the entire religion had undergone many mergers. Their leaders were called reverends, and they were allowed to marry and have kids. From all of what we read, we found them to be a very welcoming people. They had rules, of course, but as long as you were baptized, you were fully welcome to take part in their services. Rupert and I both liked that and commented that maybe they had a real good point, keeping it simple.

"Rupert?" I asked. "What do you really think He's like? I mean really, really." He knew, of course, that the "He" I was referring to was God. Rupert pondered like he always did, never rushing to say just anything because I was only a kid.

"A father," he answered simply. "A very good father." His answer stopped me and made me think. We call God our father in so many prayers, but somehow I never took it literally. But after Rupert said it, so much of what I had been wondering about seemed less confusing. I nodded, wanting him to continue, but like all good teachers (Rupert being a great one), he wanted me to do more talking than him, and I knew that he would out wait me. My head swam with thoughts that I struggled to organize. I looked at Rupert. He wasn't budging.

"Talk, child," he said. I took a deep breath

"OK," I began, "if He's our father, then He loves us like crazy."

Rupert agreed, "No argument here."

"He wants the best for us," I continued with another agreeable nod from Rupert. Then things started to get sticky. "But sometimes," I began tentatively, "sometimes we please Him and sometimes He's happy with us, but sometimes He's not."

"Sounds right," Rupert agreed. This was starting to make me uncomfortable.

"I don't like the idea that He's sometimes mad at me," I admitted.

"You're not supposed to," Rupert said. I was getting kind of troubled and started to wish that I hadn't started this conversation. I was quiet. So like all good teachers do when a student gets lost, the teacher comes for them. "Maybe mad is a little bit harsh," Rupert suggested. "Maybe He just gets a little disappointed is all." This made me feel a lot better. Don't get me wrong, I was no fan of disappointing God, but the thought of making Him really mad scared me to death. "He still loves you when you disappoint Him," Rupert explained. "He's just disappointed is all." I nodded that I understood. "He just wants you to behave is all." I nodded.

"Do you think He punishes us?" I asked. Rupert was quiet. "I mean when we do bad things, do you think He punishes us?"

"No," Rupert said firmly. "I think our own choices punish us."

"But sometimes it's hard to be good," I pointed out.

"Who says?" Rupert asked, almost aghast. "Why is it so hard?" I felt like I almost made him mad. "What does He ask that's so hard?" he challenged. I didn't know how to answer.

"Think, child," he demanded. "What does He want from us?" I was still stuck. "Think," he ordered again. "You know this." I was sure that I didn't. Rupert waited as long as he could, then he lost his patience and said, "Do I need to write it on tablets for you?"

I gasped. "The Ten Commandments," I cringed. "Sorry," I said.

Rupert shook his head. I hated disappointing him. "Recite, child," he commanded. I was nervous and prayed that those years of Sunday school wouldn't fail me.

"You shall honor no other God but me."

"You shall honor no other God but me!!!" Rupert boomed after me. "How hard is that one?"

"Not hard," I whispered with my head down.

"You bet not," Rupert almost yelled. "Next."

"You shall not misuse the name of the Lord thy God," I recited.

"Hard?" Rupert asked.

"No," I answered. He motioned for me to keep going.

"Keep the Sabbath day."

"How difficult it is to stop by once a week?'

"Not," I answered again.

"Honor your father and your mother," I added without being asked. "Not," I said before he could ask me. "Thou shall not kill."

"Not hard," Rupert answered as he began to calm down.

"Thou shall not steal."

"Not hard," we said together.

"Thou shall not commit adultery."

"Not hard for me," I answered. Rupert came close to laughing but stopped himself.

"Thou shall not bear false witness against thy neighbor," I continued.

"Telling the truth sure is easier than lying," Rupert pointed out, completely calm now.

"Thou shall not covet thy neighbor's wife."

"For sure not," Rupert nodded.

"Thou shall not covet thy neighbor's goods," I said.

"No sticky fingers," Rupert reported. I nodded.

"Now recite again from the beginning," Rupert told me. I stumbled over a couple of them. He had me list them one more time. When I was finished, he asked, "How difficult is all of that?"

"Not," I said smiling at him. I felt better about myself already.

"See, He really doesn't ask so much," Rupert pointed out. I nodded, knowing he was right.

"It's us that asks too much of Him," Rupert said. I nodded my head in agreement.

"Do you think He's funny?" I asked.

Rupert spun around. "Good Lord, child," he said, exasperated, "you sure do have a busy mind. Where did that come from?"

"I don't know," I laughed. "I was just wondering."

"Wondering if you should tell Him a joke?" Rupert asked incredulously.

"Oh, I already decided to do that," I told him honestly. Rupert looked at me with the most baffled look on his face.

"Why in the world would you want to do that?" he asked.

"Because I want to hear what His laugh sounds like," I admitted simply.

Rupert stopped walking. I stopped beside him. With one finger he turned my shoulder just a touch closer toward him and looked into my eyes with an expression that I couldn't read. It was a long look. Then he turned, and we began walking again. After a couple of minutes of silence, I became uncomfortable. "Kinda dumb, huh?" I asked, with my eyes staring down at my shoes. Rupert stopped even more suddenly than he did the first time. This time when he turned me toward him with both hands on my shoulders, he turned me squarely to face him. He looked deep in my eyes.

"Not dumb, child," he said seriously. "Not dumb at all." I nodded. I had pleased him, and it made my heart sing. We kept walking.

"But why are you so quiet?" I asked him. He shook his head back and forth. "I'm over here practicing my joke," he yelled, pretending to be exasperated. "I'm going to see him sooner than you are."

I laughed the rest of the way to the church.

The physical building of the Presbyterian church that we visited perfectly fit the welcoming description in the book we read. It was simple yet beautiful. There were no kneelers, so we sat and prayed. I introduced us, and Rupert told Him why we were there and how much we liked the place. We prayed some more and thanked Him for having us.

"Anything else?" Rupert asked me as we started to get up.

I nodded, "Yes."

Rupert sat back down. I hesitated whether to do it or not, but then I did.

"Why do elephants have trunks?" I asked to the altar. I waited the appropriate amount of time for the response, then landed the punch line, "Because they don't have any pockets to put things in!" I clutched my stomach and cracked up in the pew.

"Good golly!" Rupert hissed, grabbing me by the scruff of my neck and dragging me down the aisle. "Let's get out before He comes down and throws us out," he said. He rushed me out the door, and we spilled out onto the sidewalk laughing. Rupert collected his stones and pebbles, and we started home. Along the way we practiced the Constitution. He made me memorize the Preamble. By the time we got home, I could do it.

Lunch of cheese sandwiches and root beers, recess of *The Price Is Right*. We both lost our showcases. Rupert said he sure hoped that Bob Barker wasn't fiddling with things because he sure didn't seem that type, but it had been three days in a row without any contestants winning their showcase.

By this time we worked like a fine oiled machine, with Rupert fetching the spatula, me pushing back the furniture, and Rupert retrieving the big book. "Today is Ella Fitzgerald day," Rupert announced with his announcer's voice. I had long gotten over the fact that some of the greats were girls. Rupert assured me that a good singer can sing any song and make it his own. So after listening to the record and reading from the book, I stood atop the table and made Ella's song my own. I belted out "Take the A Train," "On the Sunny Side of the Street," and "Mack the Knife" while Rupert pounded the ivories.

And when it was three o'clock as expected, I burst out the door to where Edwin was and bid Rupert goodnight. As expected, he called, "Good night, Ella!" and laughed like crazy.

Edwin shook his head back and forth and said, "Boy, you two really are weird."

And once again I walked the entire way home laughing.

What the Heart Sees

We had worked all morning cleaning out the old shed in the back of the house. After a few hours Rupert announced that we had done enough work for the day. We settled together on the front porch to relax and play checkers with the board balancing on a small end table between us. We had our root beers and, of course, our conversation.

Every once in a while we would have to stop the game so I could run and help one of Rupert's neighbors carry their trash to the curb. It was Thursday, and garbage pickup was on Friday. Almost all of Rupert's neighbors were elderly and could use the help. They had gotten used to me being around and helping them all summer, so most of them would actually stand at their front doors or garages waiting to spot me. Rupert and I were watching for them, too, and when he saw one he would say, "You've got a customer." Then I would dart off the porch and carry their trash to the curb.

Once when I returned to the porch huffing and puffing, Rupert said, "My neighbors sure are going to miss you when school starts." I couldn't stand the thought of school starting, and it was sadly approaching fast. I nodded. I enjoyed helping Rupert's neighbors.

"Rupert," I asked him as we I made a move with my red checker, "do you think God ever comes down here?" Rupert raised an eyebrow in thought. "I mean like to check on us and stuff?"

"How would He do that?" Rupert questioned.

"By just being a regular person, a nice person, I'm sure, who just shows up for awhile when people need Him to help and guide them," I explained. "Not always, though, just sometimes."

Rupert nodded and wagged his head back and forth like this made sense to him. "Like maybe just for the summer?" He said it so matter of factly, but in a way that gave me a chill.

"What did you say?" I asked, my eyes suspiciously glued to his face. I had not been thinking of anything in particular when I asked the question, but Rupert's response inexplicably rattled me.

"Nothing," he shrugged, passing me off and not even looking up, but studying the checker board instead.

"Yes, you did," I protested. "You said, 'Like maybe for the summer.'"

"So maybe I did," he said with a small smile on his face. Then he winked at me and got up and went into the house to fill his coffee cup, leaving me speechless, my ten-year-old head spinning with thoughts out on the porch. I peeked at him through the window, watching him as he moved through the house. I pushed the thoughts out of my head.

"Ridiculous," I said aloud.

"What is?" Rupert said, suddenly beside me. I jumped, not having heard him come out the door.

"Nothing," I stammered quickly.

"Why so jumpy?" he asked.

"I'm not," I retorted too fast to be genuine.

"Looks like you've got a customer," Rupert said motioning to Mrs. Reynolds across the street. I squinted my eyes, still eyeing him warily, then hopped off the porch to help Mrs. Reynolds with her garbage. I looked up and viewed him from a distance, then shook my head and pushed the thoughts out of my head. When I got back to the porch, Rupert said, "We'll play two more games, both of which I will win, then no more checkers for the day."

"You don't know that!" I insisted.

"When are you going to understand that I know everything?" he laughed, shaking his head. The chill came back. I tried to hide my feelings, but I couldn't help but gulp and freeze for a minute.

With fake bravado, I laughed it all off. "Yeah, sure you do," I mocked. Rupert shrugged as if he didn't care if I believed him or not, which of course had me caring like crazy.

"Well," I challenged, trying to act sure of myself. "Tell me what else you know."

"Forget it," Rupert said, setting up the board for the next game. "If you don't believe in me then you don't believe in me." His carefully chosen words had me falling for this fast.

"Just tell me one more thing that you know," I demanded.

The checker board was set, and Rupert made his first move. "Well, I sure don't like being put on the spot this way," he began nonchalantly, "but I do know that I will beat you at both of these last two games, that old Snowden will be the next one out with his trash, that my phone will ring this afternoon, and that it will rain just shy of three o'clock."

I looked at him and rolled my eyes. "You do not know all of that," I said surely. "I beat you in plenty of games of checkers, any of the other neighbors could be next with their trash, that telephone of yours never rings, and the sky couldn't be bluer."

It wasn't but ten minutes later that Rupert had beaten me at both games of checkers and I sat sulking on the porch swing pushing it with the tip of my tennis shoe every other swing. He settled into his rocker and began to peruse his newspaper. He looked up over it once to smirk at me to which I responded with a bored look. This made him laugh, and his laugh annoyed me. We sat in silence with him reading and me studying his worn, wrinkly, brown face. He cleared his throat once, peeked around the newspaper and with a very condescending smile said, "I think you've got a customer." It was old Mr. Snowden waiting for me by his garage door with a full garbage bag.

I grumbled, "Don't mean nothing," as I jumped off the porch and crossed the street to help him.

When I returned to the porch, Rupert said, "Why don't you tell me what else is on your mind?"

"Nothing," I lied. He smiled at me.

"OK," he conceded. "Good to have a clear mind."

I let the silence hang over us for as long as a ten year old could, then I let him have it. "OK, if you think you know everything, then why is there bad stuff?"

"So that we appreciate the good," he answered evenly.

"Why don't all the good prayers get answered?" I shot at him.

"Because they are not part of the big plan," he said.

"Are the colors the same in heaven?"

"Prettier," he retorted without hesitation.

"Do all dogs go to heaven?"

"Absolutely."

"Do—" I was just about to fire off another question at him, but we were interrupted by the ringing of the telephone, the same telephone that had rung only one time so far this summer and even that time was a wrong number. Rupert looked at me, and our eyes locked as we listened to the next ring together.

"Excuse me," he said, smiling at me while my mouth hung open. "My telephone is ringing." I was speechless as I watched him rise from the rocker and go through the front door. I couldn't believe it. I listened as he said hello and entered into the conversation with the caller on the other end. My young head couldn't take much more. Again, I watched him through the window as he talked animatedly to whomever. My mind drifted as I studied him, but again I pushed my crazy thoughts out of my head. I went out to the edge of the porch and looked up at the sky. This is where he would be proven wrong. There was not even a cloud in the sky. When he was finished with his phone call, he came back out on to the porch with a little bit of a gloat in his smile.

"Phones ring all the time," I told him smartly.

"Agreed," he said. "Just not that one."

I had no answer for that. I sat back down on the porch swing and Rupert returned to his rocker. We sat in silence for awhile. I watched the blue sky like a hawk. A few clouds had drifted in, but certainly none that held rain. Rupert continued to read. It must have been ten minutes later when, not believing my ears, I began to hear the light thud of raindrops falling on the tin roof of the porch. My eyes nearly bulged out of my head. Rupert never lowered his paper. I jumped up and ran to the edge of the porch thinking that I must be mistaken. Putting an arm out I watched the palm of my hand fill with rain.

"Rupert!" I squealed.

"Mmmmmm?" he asked lazily. I knew he was doing this on purpose.

"Rupert!" I yelled. He put his paper down.

"Don't be yelling at me, child. I'm not deaf."

"It is raining!" I shouted. He acted as if he could care less. He was playing with me.

"Seems so," he only said. I ran to his side, grabbed his arm, and turned it so I could see his watch. It read 2:50. He had said, "Just shy of three o'clock." Rupert shook his head back and forth, acting as if he was somehow disappointed. "I'm, uhh, I mean, it's a little early."

"You said 'I'm,'" I gasped.

"Just a little slip of the tongue."

"Rupert." I whispered, staring at him without even blinking.

"Noah," he said calmly. "We can't get all shook over the rain coming a little early and, besides, lots of things are running early today." He motioned to Edwin and his friend approaching from down the street.

I couldn't stop staring at him. If I had been older, I would have probably been able to see him stifling a smile but I was, after all, only ten. Never taking my eyes off of him, I grabbed my pool bag and walked to the edge of the porch. "I'll see you tomorrow," I mumbled, trying to see if I could look right through him.

"Uh huh," he nodded. I made it down the first two steps before he called me back. When I turned to face him, his smile was huge. He took my arms and turned me toward him.

"Child," he said, still a little amused, "I'm not Him." I looked at him warily. "I've been playing checkers for seventy years. I know how to win. Old Snowden had to be next because everyone else had their trash out already, and my sister Violet calls the fourth Thursday of every month."

"The rain?" I gulped, far from convinced.

"That weather man has been saying it all morning long." He smiled at me like he thought I was cute, and all of a sudden I felt embarrassed. He took both of my hands and looked at me seriously now. "But thank you though." I grimaced sheepishly.

"You're welcome," I managed. Then looking at my shoes and feeling foolish, I said, "You're just the closest guy to Him I ever met."

Rupert lifted up my chin letting his seventy-eight-year-old wisdom-filled face look into the innocence of my ten-year-old face. He nodded and ruffled my hair. "I'll see you tomorrow," he said. I nodded.

"See you tomorrow," I promised.

One half of ten-year-old me walked home feeling silly, right next to the other half of ten-year-old me who somehow wished it was true.

God's Plans

"Rupert?" I asked, as we were on our way to the Methodist church. I had already read from the big book and now had it tucked under my arms. Neither of us knew much about Methodists, so we learned a lot. The Methodist church was started by two brothers, John and Charles Wesley. I had a brother, but we could barely take out the trash together without fighting, so I didn't think we had it in us to start a church. But anyway, the Wesley brothers were both educated men and went to Oxford University. John did his religious work through his sermons, and Charles did his through his music. The Methodists actually got their name as a joke referring to how "methodical" they were. Rupert and I both liked things orderly, so we thought we might like how the Methodists ran things.

After we walked a bit, I asked Rupert, "Do you think it's all planned out even before we get here?"

"Do you mean our lives?"

"Yeah," I told him. "Sometimes when my mother comes to tuck me into bed at night, she tells me the story of the day I was born and she always ends it by saying that God kissed me on the forehead before dropping me gently into her arms, like my life was all planned." Rupert thought for a few moments.

"Yes, I do believe you were planned," he said surely. "You were supposed to be given exactly to your mother."

"Me and only me?" I asked.

"Yes," he said. "You and only you."

"But after that," I pressed, "how much of me is planned and how much is up to me?"

Rupert laughed. "You certainly are turning into a thinker, Noah Jacob. Aren't you?"

"Well," I said, laughing back, "I just wonder things is all."

"Good job," he told me. "Intelligent people wonder things. Don't stop wondering. It makes you smarter than the rest."

"What do you think?" he asked me.

I told him, "I think we're like library books with a check-out and check-in date. God throws us down from heaven and knows the exact date we're due back. What do you think?"

"I don't rightly know," Rupert admitted.

"I saw a video one time where everyone had a timer above their head and when it reached zero, they died. But nobody could see anyone else's timer, and you couldn't see your own either," I told him.

Rupert nodded.

"I do believe that is true, and even though I never thought of it that way, we probably are walking around with timers above our heads. But I also believe that it's good that we can't see them."

"For sure," I agreed.

He nodded and asked, "Why for sure?"

I paused and thought my answer through. I found out quickly that when Rupert was teaching and I was supposed to be learning, he wanted a clear intelligent answer with good speech and even good posture. When I would answer haphazardly, he would say, "That won't get you the job." So I learned to think before speaking.

"It's better to not know, because if you know you are leaving early, you may not try so hard to make good use of your time. And if you know that you'll be here forever then, then . . ." I stammered. I realized it was the same reason. "If you know you have so much time, you'll get lazy and not make good use of your time."

"Sounds right to me," Rupert agreed with a small smile that told me that he was proud of me. For me there was no better feeling.

"Do you think that just the big things are planned or are all the tiny things planned, too?" I asked him.

"Like?" he asked.

"Like that I'll be a singer someday or get married and have three kids someday are all planned. And that I'm walking on this side of the street and not the other and that I picked Fruit Loops for breakfast were planned too."

Rupert laughed heartily. "You really, really have been thinking," he said, shaking his head. He paused, getting his own answer together. Rupert's answers always got him the job. "I'm going to say," he began, "that the singer, wife, and kids God picks, and the Fruit Loops and the side of the street you pick."

"Unless!" I squealed excitedly. "I get run over by a truck on this side of the street or choke to death on my Fruit Loops."

Rupert laughed and rolled his eyes. "I think you better stop thinking for awhile," he said.

"But for real," I giggled.

"But for real," he said. "I think we have it about figured out. Let's just say that God picks the big journey and you get to pick the paths." I smiled. I liked Rupert's theory.

"Good." I laughed and ran over to the other side of the street to walk for awhile. Rupert chuckled and shook his head again. "So we are library books," I hollered from the other side, "and we have a check out of heaven date and a due back in heaven date."

"Seems so," Rupert called back. We walked several blocks in silence. I liked thinking of life this way. It was comfortable for me. I wanted to be in charge of some of it but not all of it.

When we were nearing the church, I ran back over to the other side to join him. "One more question," I begged, knowing he had had enough for one day.

"Just one," he growled playfully.

"Do you think after we are here and gone, we ever get to come back as something else?"

"Reincarnation?!?" Rupert yelled, making me jump out of my skin. I froze and nodded.

"No," he said firmly with just the smallest smile on his face, enjoying the fact that I was scared because I knew I was in a little bit of trouble. "No," he repeated firmly again, "although God does occasionally put certain little boys on the earth to be pains in the necks of tired old men."

I laughed like crazy at this. "Oh, come on," I insisted, "I'm not that bad."

"I'll be the judge of that," Rupert grumbled as he made his way up the church steps, picking up pebbles and stones along the way and sliding them into his pocket.

"Get in there," he playfully grunted. "Let's go see what the Methodists have to say."

It was a pretty church inside. We took our front row seats. In the last churches Rupert had let me introduce us. "Hi, God. We were in the neighborhood," I explained, then paused. "And I'm not sure if you made that happen or if we did." My voice trailed off. Rupert looked sideways at me from his kneeling position with a look that said, "Move on with it."

"But anyway," I said, straightening up and getting back on track, "we somehow ended up in the neighborhood and we wanted to stop by and say hello in case you were Methodist."

Rupert nodded, satisfied, and told Him he really liked how the Methodists were running things. He told God that he liked their idea of always striving for perfection. He said we may never get to being perfect for God, but, we sure should all be trying, considering that God sure was perfect for us. I added a couple of things that I had learned from the book and liked. We sat together and said our prayer, and then spent just a few moments in the peace and quiet that can only be found in a church. Rupert thanked Him for having us, and we excused ourselves.

On the way home we studied the great artistic periods and the painters and a famous painting from each. I complained that I was positive I could live a hundred years and never need this information in real life. This got Rupert riled up enough to tell me that this was real life right now, and if I wanted lunch instead of a licking when we got home, then I better quit my griping. I shaped up right then and there, and he made me do twice as much.

"Two lessons learned at once," Rupert commented as we reached home. "Art and no back talk." I put my hands up in defeat and just nodded that I understood. Rupert chuckled at his win.

We had our cheese sandwiches and root beer for lunch, then watched *The Price Is Right*. We both won our showcases, so we were happy. Rupert was a little happier, though, because he was going to Hawaii and I was only going to Mexico.

It was Nat King Cole day, and I couldn't have been happier because I loved him. I read from the book on the blue woven carpet, then we listened and learned through the crackling, most-played record in Rupert's collection.

"Velvet," Rupert mused, wagging his head back and forth. "A voice like velvet." A few times I think I saw tears in his eyes. With my spatula in hand, atop the coffee table "I Straightened Up and Flew Right," "Nature-Boy"-ed, "Mona Lisa"-ed, and, of course, was "Unforgettable."

"Go get 'em, Mr. Cole! Rupert encouraged from the piano. "Sing it, baby," he would call. And sing I did. Three o'clock came much too soon, as always, but with feet so happy and light that they barely touched the ground, I called goodnight to Rupert.

"See you tomorrow!" I yelled as I burst out the door to an impatient Edwin.

"Mr. Cole," Rupert called after me. "What about an encore?" We laughed together—Rupert from the house and me from the sidewalk. Edwin just rolled his eyes.

An Afternoon in the Backyard

It was a Tuesday afternoon. Rupert and I were in the backyard, and I was driving him crazy. I always had the energy of a typical ten year old, but that day I somehow had even more. It was a beautiful, warm day with white puffy clouds dotting the powder blue sky. It was the kind of day that people take photos of and put on calendars—a perfect day for an old man to sit in a chair beneath an apple tree with his body outstretched and his eyes closed and his face turned toward to the sun, soaking up the warmth because, as he said, "his old bones needed it to bring them back to life." But this particular old man had a pesky ten year old to contend with, and, as always, I was on the go and chattering. I was exhausting Rupert but not myself.

Rupert had already banned me from the tire swing that he had put up for me at the beginning of the summer in the large, old oak tree in the back of the yard. Instead of swinging on it like I should have, I insisted on spinning it around in a circle as fast as I could, then trying to dive through the middle of it. Rupert insisted that I was going to do nothing more than hang myself, so I wasn't allowed on it for the rest of the day. I moved from there to the uneven fence that ran around the perimeter of the yard. My goal was to walk, balance-beam-style, around the length of the fence without falling. I wasn't even close to being able to do it. Rupert kept glancing up from his relaxing to catch me falling off the right side and then off the left side. Finally, I slipped and fell dangerously right down the middle. "Off!!" he ordered, and I was banned from the fence for the day.

My next challenge was the apple tree. I loved climbing trees, and I was good at it since I was small and light, allowing me to climb higher than most. I was determined to pick the juiciest, reddest apples for Rupert and me to eat. Rupert was sitting below watching me. I would choose one, pull it gently from the branch and toss it down to him. With his pocket knife, Rupert would carefully peel it, trying to keep the apple skin in one long curling piece. Three apples later he had not succeeded; all of the skins had broken. I was determined that we needed to try just one more. Rupert glanced up at me from his peeling and warned, "Not too high. Back down a little bit. Careful, careful." All the while my ten-year-old lack of sense was insisting that I knew what I was doing. I was making Rupert nervous, and he was getting ornery.

"Get down," he finally ordered.

"But I found the perfect one," I protested, eyeing the reddest, roundest apple dangling precariously at the end of a high branch.

Rupert sighed. "It will fall when it is ready," he told me, rising from the chair and positioning himself under the tree.

"But if it falls on its own, it will get bruised," I argued. "I want to pick it while it's perfect."

"Down," he ordered again.

"Please," I begged. "I know I can get it. I'll get down as soon as I get just this last one."

I could tell Rupert was getting mad and would have loved to have taken a swat at me if only I were within reach, but I was safely (or unsafely depending on how you looked at it) ten feet above him.

"That branch is too thin to hold you," Rupert warned as I wiggled further out on to it. He was standing directly beneath me now with his arms raised in the air. "Noah, down!" he shouted.

"I've got it," I groaned, reaching one final time out onto the branch to grab the apple. Of course, just as I did, the branch bent underneath my weight, and I tumbled headfirst into the open air and directly into Rupert's waiting arms.

"Yeah, you know what you're doing," he growled, setting me upright on to the ground. "Now, no more tree!!" he collapsed back into his chair.

"Sorry," I said sheepishly, "but look how perfect it is." I handed him the apple. "This will be our lucky one," I said. "You'll peel the skin all in one piece, and we'll get our million dollars." I was referring to a game that we played when we peeled apples. We had decided that if Rupert could peel off the whole skin in one piece, then we would get a million dollar prize. So far that summer we had never won.

"It's the million dollar apple, Rupert," I told him.

"Let me see it," he said, softening up a bit as he took it from me.

"It is a beautiful one," he admitted, examining it. He took out his knife and began to work. As he did, I began doing cartwheel after cartwheel in a giant circle around the tree and the chair. I was still driving him crazy, but at least I was on the ground.

"Rupert," I asked him in between cartwheels, "do you think I'm weird?"

He looked up and frowned. "No, I do not think you are weird," he said emphatically. Then, trying to lighten the mood, he clarified, "A pain in the neck? Yes. Weird? No."

I must have still looked troubled because he told me to come closer. I stopped cart wheeling and plopped myself at his feet.

"What brought this on?" he asked. I started off by saying, "Nothing," just like kids always do, but because it was Rupert, I told him about what happened the night before.

"Well, you know how I like to stand on my bed and sing and pretend I'm performing for a crowd into my mirror?"

"Mmmmm," he nodded. "So?"

"Well, until last night nobody but me and you knew that."

"OK," he encouraged. Then I told him the whole story.

Like every other day, I raced home to perform on my stage to my crowd of thousands. The way it always worked was, when dinner was ready, someone would always pound loud enough on the ceiling below to make me hear it through the noise of the tape player—my band. I would bid the crowd in whatever city I was in on that particular night (of course I kept a map and push pins tacked up on the inside of my closet door to keep track of my globe trotting), "Good night!"

I'd thank them for their undying love, support, and appreciation, and as I jumped down the steps to dinner (my awaiting private jet) with the chanting of them begging for an encore, I would apologize and hop onto my seat at the kitchen table—my plane. Well, last night I got caught. I guess the music was too loud, and I didn't hear the pounding on the ceiling. Without warning the bedroom door flung open so harshly that it slammed against the wall behind it. My father filled the door frame. I was caught cold—standing on the bed, holding onto my hair brush, and facing the mirror with Tony Bennett in the background. I stood frozen in place for a moment, then I turned toward my father. Our eyes locked, neither of us knowing what to say. He blinked first. I swallowed hard, having no idea what was coming next. He walked to the dresser and pressed stop on the tape player. My eyes widened as he took one step closer to the bed. His face was unreadable. He pointed to the bed with a sagging finger.

"What's that?"

I dropped my head and stared at my big toe poking out of my white gym sock.

"My stage," I whispered.

He nodded.

"And that?" he asked, pointing toward my hairbrush.

"My microphone," I said, It was barely audible because I had been holding my breath.

"And that?" he asked, pointing to the mirror.

I let the air out of my lungs and through my nose and mouth.

"The camera," I said, knowing my face couldn't be redder. I couldn't look at him but could feel him walk a few more steps around my bed. I stood frozen.

He walked behind me and squinted into the mirror, tilting his head to see what I was seeing from my vantage point. Then he turned and walked out of the room, leaving the door open. I let myself breathe again and dropped to a sitting position onto the bed. I sat with my legs tucked under me, my mind swirling with a million jumbled thoughts.

Afraid to move, my heart jolted, then began to beat wildly as I heard his footsteps pounding their way back up the stairs. I had no idea what he was going to do or say. I was embarrassed and terrified. What did fathers do to weird kids?

At first I didn't raise my head, but I could see him out of the corner of my eyes. He had brought his toolbox with him and set it on the floor. He unpacked his tools, and then I did raise my head to watch as he methodically and carefully unscrewed the mirror from the wall. He was taking my camera away. I lowered my head, embarrassed. I was a weird kid. Carefully, he set the mirror alongside the dresser. I was expecting him to repack his tools and carry the mirror out of the room. But instead I watched as he unpacked a drill and drilled four new holes into the wall above where the old ones were. I watched as he carefully carried the mirror back over to its spot above the dresser, remounting it about eight inches higher on the wall. I watched his back and the balding back of his head as he repacked his tools neatly in the box, then latched it shut. He picked the toolbox up and walked again to the other side of the bed and viewed his work. He tilted his head from one side to the other, making sure it was straight, looking satisfied with his work. He turned and looked at me. I looked back with my ten-year-old face.

"Your camera needs to be higher for your audience to see you," he said. I nodded, never taking my eyes off of him. He was right; I had grown. In the last months I had needed to stoop to see myself in the mirror. He walked out of the room with the tool box in one hand, closing the bedroom door with the other. I listened as the sound of his footsteps disappeared. I reached over to the tape player, pressed play, picked up my microphone, stood up on my stage, looked into the camera, and sang my heart out again.

When I was done sharing my story, I turned over in the grass with my head propped up on my hands and faced Rupert for his reaction. Rupert was quiet for awhile, then he looked at me calmly. "You are not weird," he said again. "And you may not be old enough to realize that although good parents don't always understand their children, they always love them—and you have good parents."

Maybe I couldn't understand all of it, but I did understand some. I told him that they both came into my room last night and gave me an extra hug. Rupert nodded in a way that said that he knew he was right. "Maybe tonight," he suggested, "it might be a good idea for you to give the extra hugs good night." I promised that I would.

"And one more thing," he said, holding up the longest strand of apple skin that I had ever seen. "I think we just won a million dollars." Together we laughed.

I laid back in the grass, finally calm, and watched as Rupert split the apple in two. In the silence, we enjoyed our apple, the beautiful day, and the peace of an understanding friendship, realizing that what we had found in each other was much better than a million dollars.

The Final Exam

It was the last day of summer vacation. "Now there will be none of that," Rupert scolded when I walked into the house trying to hide the tears in my eyes. "We're not spending our last summer day together moping around and being sad." But for a moment we both caught a glimpse of each other's sad eyes. In spite of our fake bravado, we both knew that something very special was coming to an end.

"Where are we going today?" I asked him. I thought maybe he had one last church visit planned for us.

"Just one quick outing," he said, "if we have the time. Otherwise just a quiet day at home."

"Why wouldn't we have time?" I asked him.

"Well, you've got to get to your final exam," he said.

"My what?" I all but screeched.

"Every school year ends with a final exam," he explained. "How else will we know if you learned anything?"

I couldn't believe my ears. "You never said anything about a final exam," I pointed out nervously.

"Noah," he said sarcastically, "there's a final exam."

"Very funny," I said. "Is it long? Is it hard?" I was beginning to get genuinely rattled.

"That depends on you," he said, taking me by the arm and leading me to the kitchen table and shoving me into a chair.

"Depends on how hard you really studied, if you really listened or not, if you learned anything at all," he said disappearing into the other room.

"You saw me!" I called stubbornly over my shoulder to wherever he went. "I learned lots."

"You were only supposed to learn one thing," he yelled from somewhere in the house. Now I was really getting anxious. I could hear him in the closet rummaging around. "The rest was just time fillers," he called.

"Maybe you could have told me that!" I yelled, then suddenly jumped when he appeared out of nowhere beside me. He had something in his hands that he held behind his back.

"Close your eyes," he ordered. I obeyed. I could hear him set two things on the table in front of me. One made a small thudding sound and the other was set down with a clang.

"Open," he told me. What I found on the table were two items. One was his wristwatch, a worn but beautiful watch that he once told me had been passed down in his family from father to son. The other was the most beautiful thing I had ever seen. I blinked, unsure of whether to trust my eyes or not. After staring long enough I knew that I could. It was a stone sculpture of the face of God. I couldn't help but rub my eyes and blink again. It was undeniably Him. It was always a little startling to me to know that some people were able to create paintings, sketches, and even sculptures like this one that depicted God even though it was a mystery as to what God looked like. These artists could render an image of God so perfectly that we all would know who it was. Now the incredible thing about his sculpture was that it was made of the concrete, pebbles, and slivers of rocks that Rupert had taken from each of the churches that we had visited that summer.

"Rupert," I said to him in a stunned voice that was barely audible. "It's beautiful!" I slowly shook my head back and forth. "Really, really beautiful."

He smiled. I could tell he was proud.

"How in the world could you make something so beautiful?" I asked him in genuine awe.

"Nothing but a little imagination and glue," he said simply. I reached my hand toward the sculpture, but this was a mistake because he slapped my hand away before I could even get close. "No touching," he admonished. "You don't need to touch it to complete the exam." He saw me eyeing the watch. "And this," he said, moving the watch away from me with one finger to the other side of the table, "you get if you pass the exam." My mouth dropped open. "In my day," he explained, "people gave other people timepieces as gifts to remember time well spent together."

"So this will remind me of our summer," I said sadly.

"I suspect," Rupert said.

"Actually," he continued raising an eyebrow, "if you pass the test, you get to keep both of them." My mouth dropped open a second time. There was nothing I wanted more than that watch and that sculpture.

"So you're ready for the test?" Rupert laughed.

"Totally," I told him. Now I was motivated. "Bring it on! Where is it?"

"It isn't anywhere," Rupert chuckled. "No sense in writing it down, considering it's only one question."

"OK. OK," I said, letting the fact that this bothered me slide by. "What's the question?"

Rupert by this time was very amused. "The question is," he said with a small smile on his face, "What does it mean?"

"It's the face of God," I answered quickly and excitedly, sure that I had gotten it right. I was so proud of myself that I jumped out of the chair and reached for both the watch and the sculpture. Again I got another slap.

"I didn't ask, 'What is it?'" Rupert whispered, getting my attention more than he ever did when he raised his voice. "I asked, 'What does it mean?'" I sat back down and settled into the chair. I sighed. Obviously, this was going to require some more thought. I settled even further into the chair and sighed louder, which made Rupert laugh as he walked out of the room and onto the porch. "Call me when you're ready," he said as he settled into the rocker with his pipe. "We do have one place to go today if you get done in time and pass the test."

"What if I don't?" I squealed in genuine panic. I could hardly stand the thought of not only failing the test, but also not getting either the watch or the sculpture.

"I suspect you will do just fine," Rupert said matter-of-factly from the porch.

I checked the clock on the wall; it was 10:02. "OK. OK," I whispered to myself, "just calm down and think. You can do this." I stared at God, and He stared at me. The beauty of it astounded me. The intricate detail that Rupert was able to capture by piecing the stones together was amazing. It was a true work of art. I checked the clock again, 10:25. I had nothing. I saw its beauty but not its meaning. I could hear the creak back and forth of the porch rocker as Rupert relaxed on the porch. I got caught up in watching the shadows of the slats in the chair sway to and fro along the wall. I actually started feeling sleepy, then I shook myself and tried to refocus and scolded myself to concentrate. I stared and stared.

At 11:00 I got up from the chair and walked around the table slowly inspecting the sculpture from each side. "What does it mean?" I muttered to myself. I was so lost in my thoughts that I hadn't noticed Rupert coming into the kitchen. I jumped when I saw him.

"I didn't touch it!" I said quickly.

"Didn't say you did," he answered me, pouring himself a cup of coffee.

"And by the way," he said, leaving the room and heading toward the porch, "you get only one chance to get the answer right."

I groaned and sat back down. I might as well say goodbye to the sculpture and the watch. I was never going to get them. And if there was one thing I learned about Rupert Holmes, it was that he was not the kind of man to give me something I didn't earn. The clock said 11:33, and I still had nothing. I tried to concentrate on only the sculpture, but instead my mind just kept wandering to the past months—how my summer had started so badly that night in the kitchen with my parents forcing me to go to the pool with Edwin, and then how it all turned itself around the very next day when I met Rupert. I thought back on all of our days together. I replayed the Monday visits to the churches and learning about the faithful people who went there: the Catholics, the Mormons, the Baptists, the Presbyterians, the Methodists, the Jews. I thought back on them and all of the other religious people that we read and talked about at home. I thought back on all the miles we walked together that now seemed like just a few steps. I thought back on reading from the big music book on the blue woven rug and singing from the coffee table. My eyes smarted and I realized, even at such a young age, that it had been the best summer of my life and would probably be better than any other that I would ever have. I couldn't help it then; my eyes filled with tears, and I cried into my own hands. And as the tears flowed, the answer finally came to me.

"Rupert, I'm ready," I choked out. The clock read 12:00. I heard the creak of the rocker slow and watched the shadow on the wall stop. He came into the kitchen. I stood up and cleared my throat just like I knew he would want.

Then I began, "The sculpture is the face of God made out of the stones from all of the different churches that we visited. It means that there is only one God for all of us. It means that God isn't any one particular religion; He actually is all of the religions put together. And when we get to heaven, we will see that He is the combination of all religions. It doesn't matter what church we belong to down here, we will all be one up there. God isn't just some of us, He is all of us. And even though we divide ourselves up into different groups, when we get to heaven He will put us all back together and make us understand that when we see His face, we are all one. We are all really just Believers. And that is what matters."

I was done. The kitchen was quiet except for the faint ticking of Rupert's watch. I looked up at his face, praying that my answer was right. His eyes were closed and when he opened them, I couldn't tell for sure, but it looked like there might be tears in them. Then he looked down at me and simply said, "Good boy." No words could ever be sweeter; no words had ever meant more to me. I had made him proud. "Good boy," he said again as he picked up the watch and wrapped it around my wrist, then took the sculpture and placed it gently into my swim bag. I didn't notice until we were leaving the kitchen that he had nailed my spatula to the kitchen wall, putting it on display. "I get to keep that," he said matter-of-factly, "although I don't know why I'd want to." Then he laughed. I followed him out of the front door.

"Where are we going?" I asked.

He said only, "You'll see. It's got to be a quick one. We've got to get back in time for *The Price Is Right*." I nodded and, instead of asking again, I just walked happily beside him. I didn't really care where we were going. It didn't matter as long as I was with him. He walked us into town, directly to the movie theater. As we walked through the front door, the ticket vendor asked if she could help us. Rupert tipped his hat and said, "No, thank you," and walked us directly to the photo booth. I laughed as he fished coins from his pockets. Knowing what was next, he pushed the curtain back and climbed inside. I climbed in after him, and, with me sitting on his lap, we smiled together for the camera. The bulb flashed, taking pictures of two of the most unlikely best friends. With a strip of photos for him and one for me, we walked back to the house. I put mine safely in my bag. I swelled with pride as Rupert put his on the mantle next to the framed photos of Ruby and Lilac.

We ate a late lunch—cheese sandwiches and root beer, of course. This time I bit the caps off of the bottles and handed him one before sliding the caps into my pocket. My lunch never tasted better. I knew that no matter what I would have for lunch at school I would be missing my cheese sandwich and my root beers. One last time we clinked the bottles together. I had saved every single bottle cap. We watched *The Price Is Right*. We both won our showcases and decided that we would share the cars, split the money, and go on the trips together. We spent the rest of the afternoon lazily relaxing on the porch with the record player pushed up to the open window playing our favorites. Rupert sat with me on the porch swing instead of sitting on his rocker. He tucked me under his arm and gently rocked the swing back and forth. I wanted to stay that way forever. We hardly moved from the swing—getting up once to get the mail and a second time to sit by the pond for awhile.

Several times Rupert tried to joke with me. "Sixth grade," he spontaneously announced, "that's big time." He laughed. "Before you know it, you'll be seventy-eight and sitting on your porch all day long."

"I wish I already was," I sulked.

"No wishing life away," Rupert reminded me. "Too much living to do before sitting." I nodded.

"Rupert," I asked, "what do you think will come of me?"

"How do you mean?" he asked.

"I don't know," I said, having a difficult time putting it into words. "I mean just everything."

"Well," he began thoughtfully, "first, I think you'll go out there and take care of your business in sixth grade. That's what you'll do with everything. You're strong. You'll take what life gives you—good and bad."

"Like you did," I noted. He nodded and took a drag from his pipe.

"Go to school as long as you can," he told me. I agreed.

"Rupert," I asked tentatively, "will I have music?" He paused.

"Do you want music?" he asked.

"More than anything in the world," I admitted.

He smiled and with a gleam in his eye he said, "The music's coming, boy. Trust me on this one. The music's coming." I perked up and smiled. "I already heard from someone on this one." he grinned, casting his eyes upward. I grinned too, not doubting him at all.

"He told you?" I laughed.

"Long ago," Rupert smiled. "I was just waiting for you to ask." I leaned back and took a moment to imagine myself as one of the great singers that we had enjoyed listening to that summer.

"Just promise me something," he said quietly, interrupting my daydream. "Promise me you'll always remember where you came from and who you are." I nodded, promising. "Who are you?" he asked me. I knew the answer. He had taught me well.

"I am Noah Jacob, and I am a Believer," I told him surely. This time Rupert nodded.

"You say it too," I told him.

He smiled. "I am Rupert Holmes, and I am a Believer."

All day I watched the clock like it was my enemy. At 3:00 my heart sank clear to the bottom of my stomach and I think Rupert's did too, as we watched Edwin and his friend approaching from the distance. Silently he helped me gather my things. He told me not to cry, but this time I didn't obey. Looping my swim bag over my shoulders for me, he stood me in front of him and held my shoulders. "Not goodbye," he reminded me. "This is just see you later."

"Saturday," I told him. "Not later." We had decided that I would still come and visit on Saturdays.

"Saturday," Rupert confirmed, "Only a few days away." He smiled through sad eyes. "Our time together will only be sweeter." Rupert was always saying things like that that overflowed with wisdom. He poked me in the stomach. I threw myself into his arms. I was swallowed in his warm, loving hug.

"I love you, Rupert Holmes," I whispered fiercely.

"I love you, Noah Jacob," he whispered back.

He let go first, knowing that I never would. "Go child," Rupert ordered.

"See you Saturday," I said softly. I walked down the steps to the sidewalk. Rupert stood on the porch and stayed there while I walked backwards down the street, waving the entire time. Neither of us ever turned away.

Summer Ends

The first days back at school were difficult. I wore the watch that Rupert gave me and looked at it constantly. It reminded me so much of him—the old elegant styling, the masculine gold, the straight and narrow lines, the old-fashioned numbers. I would watch the hands tick along, slow and steady, and be reminded of the way Rupert lived. But as much as the watch made me happy, it also made me sad, because when I looked at the time I couldn't help but imagine what we would be doing at that time if it were still summer—relaxing on the porch, visiting a church, or singing in the living room. Even at my young age, I knew what a double-edged sword was. I loved the watch because it reminded me of him, but it also brought me pain because all I wanted was for it to be the same time on a different day.

But it was already Wednesday, just a couple of days until Saturday. I had been sleep-walking through the first days. Some of my friends asked me what was wrong, but they were used to me being kind of spacy. I spent my time in class gazing out the window, daydreaming of Rupert sitting on the wooden rocker in the front porch or eating his lunch at the kitchen table. A couple of my teachers made comments like, "Summer is over, Noah." Or, "Come on, Noah, let's get with it." I just looked blankly at them. No one could understand.

My parents also commented that I was being a little quiet. "Was school OK today?" my mother would ask. When I assured her that everything was fine, she left me alone. When you have five kids, you really can't spend a lot of time on just one, and I was the quiet one anyway. No one noticed the watch, either, which happily surprised me. I wanted it to be a secret that only I could see.

It was Wednesday night at dinner. My older sister was arguing with my mother over the length of a skirt she had bought. My father was saying, "Listen to your mother"—his favorite words of wisdom. My little sisters, who had a language all their own, were playing some weird string game while eating, and my older brother, who was two years older than me and already twenty pounds heavier, was ignoring everyone and eating like a machine.

"That black man over on Tenth Street passed away," my mother said casually to my father. He grunted and nodded. It was so inconsequential that she was already getting ready to talk about something else.

"Wait!" I shouted so loudly that it made everybody stop and look at me. "Wait!" I repeated, not caring. "What did you say?"

My mother looked confused. "Nothing really," she said. "I was just telling your father that the old black man that lived on Tenth passed." I know that I was staring at her with eyes wider than they'd ever been, and my heart was pounding wildly, and I was sweating, shaking. Please tell me she didn't mean what I thought she meant.

"What do you mean, passed?" I demanded. My brother stopped eating just long enough to roll his eyes at me.

"Like dead," said my sister who is usually not sarcastic but was still angry over the skirt. I ignored her and looked back at my mother with pleading eyes. My mother may not have always understood me, but she always knew how I felt.

"I mean he died, honey," she said quietly. "On Monday," she continued. "Mrs. Martin said his family came yesterday, and they'll be burying him tomorrow." I could tell she was completely confused by my outburst. My breathing became shallow. The jabbering of my little sisters was making my already spinning head spin faster. I took in a gulp of air so I wouldn't pass out.

"Can I please be excused?" I blurted out. My mother looked at my untouched food, then at my father. He nodded.

"Honey, we didn't even know him," she offered softly. I got up from the table in a trance and walked out of the kitchen.

"He's just so sensitive," I heard my father say in response to my mother's apparently questioning look. I could almost see him shrug.

The rest of their conversations echoed in my ears. "Leave it up to Noah," my sister said, "to care about a guy he doesn't even know."

"He's weird," my brother added. The chattering of my little sisters continued on between their comments.

"Why do you think a man like that would want to stay here?" my mother questioned my father. "I mean I think he was the only black man on this side of town. You'd think he would want to be with his family." I could picture my father nodding, shrugging, and continuing to eat.

"Maybe he was with his family," was all I could mutter to myself as I reached the top step, walked into my bedroom, closed the door, and fell onto my bed. With my face in my pillow, I cried the tears of my first broken heart.

That night I waited for the house to get quiet. My mother came in to check on me once and to say goodnight. I listened as the chaos of showers, homework, teeth brushing, and the last of the sibling arguments of the day slowed and then stopped. One by one I could tell my little sisters were in bed, my older sister and older brother had retreated to their rooms, and my mother had gone to her bedroom to read. The only sound that I could hear was the muffled conversation on the TV that my father was watching downstairs. He was surely asleep with the remote in his hand.

I opened the bedroom window, climbed out onto the porch roof and jumped down to the grass below. Although it was ten o'clock at night, it was still warm from the Indian summer we'd been having. I had to get to Rupert's. I walked at a normal pace, wanting to get there but at the same time fearing what I might find. And when I did get there, the first thing I saw sickened me. There was a "For Sale" sign in the front yard. My stomach squeezed.

The next thing I noticed was the huge pile of garbage set out for the trash. I dared to walk closer. There was just enough light streaming down from the streetlight above for me to see that almost all of Rupert's things had been piled on the edge of the grass. The glow of the light fell upon Rupert's now broken rocking chair that had been thrown on top of the porch swing.

I knelt down and looked closer at one of the open boxes and could see just the tip of something poking out from under a stack of dishes. It was the handle of the spatula microphone. I pulled it out. I saw a box of clothes with just a snag of cloth sticking out. I yanked at it and found it was Rupert's "going to church shirt." I pulled it free of the box and hugged it to my chest. It still smelled of him. I wondered where his Bible had gone. To me, it felt as if his entire life had been thrown to the curb.

Peering from behind the pile, I could see the silhouettes of a man and a woman sitting inside of the living room. I wondered who they were. My eyes filled with tears as I realized it wasn't Rupert's house anymore. Clutching the spatula and the shirt, I turned and walked back home. I shimmied up the porch roof into the window of my bedroom. Without undressing, I crawled into the bed sweating and dirty, still clutching the shirt and the spatula. It took hours for my breathing to become regular and for my heart to slow down. This time, lying there, I was too numb and sad to cry.

Saying Goodbye

The next morning I stuffed my church shirt and my tie in my backpack and rode the bus to school as usual. When the bus unloaded, I made sure that I was in the middle of the crowd, blending in with them. When everyone walked right toward the school doors, I went left. Sneaking around the back of the bus, I slipped away into the woods. It took me about an hour to walk all the way back into town where Rupert's church was. When I got there, several people were filing in. I snuck behind a Dumpster and changed out of my school shirt and into the dress collar church shirt and tie. I tucked in the shirt and tried to smooth the wrinkles out. I wanted to look my best. I know Rupert would have looked his best for me.

I scrambled as I heard the opening hymn, stuffing the school clothes back into my backpack and tossing it behind the Dumpster. I would come back for it later. I had planned on sneaking into the church at the very last minute anyway. I climbed the huge concrete steps to the front door and pulled just a hair on the heavy wooden door and peeked through the crack. What I saw was a handful of people, fewer than I thought Rupert deserved. Some I recognized; some I didn't. Old Mr. Snowden was there along with Miss Margaret, the casserole lady, as well as a few other neighbors who I didn't know by name.

Sitting in the front row was a lady that could be only one person—Rupert's sister, Violet. Rupert's words still rang in my ears, "You'll know Violet when you see her, pretty as a picture she is, but God surely did give her the only body he could to accommodate her great big heart." Violet was a gigantic woman. All dressed in black with tears streaming down her face, she was fanning herself with one of the hymnals. Next to her was a younger black man who I guessed was her son. He was dressed respectfully in a black suit and showed no expression on his face as Violet held onto his arm. I realized very quickly that there were not enough people in the church for me to hide in the back. I knew then that I wasn't going to be able to go inside. My heart sank. I felt cowardly because Rupert would have walked proudly through an army of people for me. But I was just a kid, and how could I explain my being there? My heart could, of course, but I would have never been able to put it into words. I must have accidentally pulled on the door a little more and the creaking sound caused some of the people to turn. Frightened, I let the door go and ran to the side of the church. As I did, I could hear the sound of someone pulling the door tightly closed, firmly shutting me out.

Out of breath and scared, I found myself underneath an open window. A stained glass panel of a shepherd holding a staff and guiding a sheep was above me. The window was open about a foot, so I was able to hear every word. I sat with my back pressed against the rough concrete wall, my arms wrapped around my legs, and my chin tucked between my knees. I took part in each part of the service just as if I were inside, and I let my tears fall freely down my face. Somehow I felt closer to Rupert where I sat than if I had been inside. Somehow it felt private, almost like it was just the two of us.

When the service was over, I knew that they would be going to the gravesite next. I stayed where I was, out of sight. The people spilled out of the front door in groups. Most remained quiet as they stood about, delaying getting into their own cars before taking Rupert to his final resting place. The men stood solemnly, and the women whispered about whatever women whisper about at these times. I caught another glimpse of Violet. I remembered how Rupert would laugh and his eyes would gleam when he spoke of her. "Only family besides my ma and pa," he once said, "that I ever had any use for." Then he would laugh again, and I could tell he was letting his mind drift off to a private place or memory. Then he would mutter, "Yes, sir, my sister is one that always truly loved me." Then he would say the words, "My Violet," with such love that hearing him, no one could ever doubt that he truly loved her.

I peered around the corner of the building, watching the people, wondering if this was how it always was when someone died. People would show up at the service and pay their respects, and I appreciated that. But in a few hours each of them would simply go back to their owns lives, and not one thing would be different for them. But I, on the other hand, would be left behind with a hole not only in my heart but in my life as well.

I was just getting ready to inch back away further out of sight when I heard a boisterous laugh come from the sidewalk. "That's what my Rupert would say," I heard Violet comment as she made her way down the sidewalk. The people cleared her path like the parting of the sea and allowed her large body to pass through on her way to the limousine door that someone had just scurried to open. "Yep, that's what my Rupert would say." She laughed again, the biggest belly laugh I had ever heard coming from the biggest specimen of a person that I had ever seen. I gulped as I realized that I had heard that laugh before. She had the same laugh as Rupert.

She lumbered from side to side when she walked, and I swear the sidewalk was quaking as she did. Every single part of her from her many chins down to her huge belly to her monstrous legs jiggled and rolled as she moved. The tires of the limousine sank a good four inches as she heaved herself inside. Someone had to push on her just a bit to make sure she was all in before shutting the door. By this time Rupert had been loaded into the back. The others got into their cars, and the procession slowly drove away. I came out of my place of hiding, looking up and down the street, trying to decide which of the three cemeteries they were headed for. They made a left at the end of the block which narrowed it down to two. And then Rupert spoke to me. I remembered him making mention to me once, for no reason at all, that "I'll be fine when I'm resting atop my hill." I realized then that he was making reference to his passing, and with those words I knew just which cemetery they were headed for.

I took off running to catch up to the funeral precession. I caught up to them, huffing and puffing and out of breath, at the Baptist cemetery at the very edge of town. I spotted the cars at the very bottom of the biggest hill. It was a perfect spot, and that mattered to me. I knew that Rupert had chosen it himself because one time when I watched him rearrange some papers in his desk, I saw a folder that had the name of the cemetery on it.

I took a deep breath and began to climb the steep hill. I would go only as close as I could without letting them see me, but I wanted to be close enough to hear. I found a spot off to the right of where they were gathered and lay flat on my stomach so they couldn't see me, but I was close enough to hear. I could see the casket. It was perfect. It looked like a piece of deep, dark, cherry furniture, new but somehow ageless at the same time. Its lacquered finish glistened in the sun. It sat elegant and proud, just like Rupert. And if he had to be in a box, that was the kind of box he should be in. I watched as they lowered it from its metal casters into the hole below, and the preacher tossed one shovel of dirt on top. I had seen this in movies but never in person, and seeing it now made me hold my breath. As men with shovels continued to fill in the rest of the hole, the preacher recited the concluding prayers.

Then he pronounced what were the saddest words I had ever heard in my whole ten years: "Here lies dear Rupert William Holmes, gone now from this world forever." I lay on my stomach with the grass staining my church shirt and my hands burying my face, sobbing for my best friend.

When the gravesite service was over, I stayed in my perch just on the crest of the hill and let Rupert's family, friends, and neighbors work their way down the hill. When they were all gone and I was alone, I stood quietly before the mound of dirt. It was still just a pile and hadn't been raked yet and that bothered me. After staring at it for awhile, I finally dropped to my knees and began to rake it with my fingers into some sort of shape. I tried to make it into the rectangle that I thought it should be. I worked intently, letting my tears fall into the fresh earth.

When I was satisfied with my efforts, I laid down with him, turning from my back to my stomach. I felt comfort and peace just being with him. I checked the time on Rupert's watch and realized I had better get going. I had left my backpack at the church and needed to go back and get it, then get back to school to catch the bus back home. I stood up and wiped the dirt off of my pants and shirt. I gazed one long last look at the mound of dirt and couldn't help but think how it was odd how we lay people to rest—not something you think about until the mound of dirt covers someone you love. I had a difficult time just turning and walking away. Would Rupert just walk away from me? Probably, I suppose. The living don't seem like they have much choice. I couldn't bring myself to say goodbye, so instead I simply said, "I'll see you tomorrow, Rupert. . . . I'll see you tomorrow. . . ."

I slowly walked back to the church. When I got there, I crawled behind the Dumpster and fished out my backpack. I could hear music being played low somewhere nearby. I walked along the side of the church and realized that it was coming from the basement of the church. It took me a minute to realize that it was Rupert's wake. Rupert's family and friends had all come back here. I cautiously approached a half-open window and peered inside. The people inside were eating, drinking, and mingling in the simple basement, sitting at long rectangular tables. It didn't seem proper to me. It seemed proper for everyone to go home and be sad, not to go have a party and eat fried chicken, baked beans, potato salad, and cake. But I was too tired and numb to care at that point. I turned from the window and started to walk away when something snagged my shirt sleeve and startled me. I jumped away and tumbled to the ground.

"Gotcha!" I heard a voice say. It was Violet.

"Get off the ground, child," she ordered. But before I could obey, she pulled me up easily by one arm. She began dusting me off.

"Who are you, child?" she asked gently. "You've been following us all day." I was silent in fear.

I swallowed. "I'm nobody," I finally managed, my voice hoarse.

"You're not nobody!" she exclaimed. "Were you a friend of my dear Rupert?" she asked. I nodded.

"Wait," she said, a sudden look of recognition coming to her eyes. She pulled Rupert's miniature Bible out of the pocket of her dress, and out of the Bible she took three photos. They were the photos from the mantle. One was of Ruby, one was of Lilac, and the other was the strip of photos of Rupert and me from the movie theater booth.

"You're not nobody, child," she insisted. "You're Noah Jacob." My eyes widened, and I gasped at her knowing my name. "He loved you, child," she said, looking directly into my eyes, "as much as he would have loved one of his own," I nodded, my eyes welling with tears at her words. She looked down at me sadly.

"Leave it to my Rupert to find a scrawny baby bird like you and nurse him." She shook her head back and forth.

"He was my friend," I managed in a voice that came out in an almost inaudible croak instead of even a whisper. Her face was so kind and knowing.

"Of course he was, child, and you were his friend, too," she said surely. "Did you love him?" she asked, but I knew that she already knew my answer. The tears spilled down my cheeks.

"And how he loved you," she repeated firmly, knowing I needed to hear it again.

I nodded.

"But we're done crying over my Rupert," she said almost scolding me and my tears. "We're now left to celebrating him," she continued, motioning back to the basement.

"Dry those," she ordered. I obeyed and wiped the tears from my cheeks.

"You're Violet," I dared to say. Her entire face lit with surprise, letting it register that Rupert had mentioned her. She stared at me, looking right through me. I know she was trying to figure out just how Rupert and I came to be.

"I am," she said proudly. "I am." She said it in a way that announced that being Rupert Holmes' sister was indeed something to be proud of. And I liked this. I agreed with her.

"He loved you a lot," I managed shyly, then looked at my dirty shoes.

"I know, child" she said softly. Then her voice boomed. "Child, do people feed you?" Her loud voice made me jump. "I have never seen such a scrawny little white boy. Pale too." She made me feel a little ashamed for not being bigger. "Do you have people?" It took me a minute to realize that she meant family. I nodded. "Good people?" she asked suspiciously. I wagged my head again.

She paused again, taking this all in, then suddenly she grabbed me by the arm and said again, "Now we are left to celebrate our Rupert." She pulled me toward the basement door. I was scared and didn't want to go in there, but when I opened my mouth to protest no sound came out. The next thing I knew I was in the basement of the church with too many pairs of eyes staring at me. She pushed me in a chair so hard that it slid across the floor a few inches before it settled with me in it. She pulled a chair up for herself, and I watched it disappear underneath her.

"Lily!" she yelled over her shoulder. "Bring me a plate." Violet pulled my chair up close to hers, then proceeded to feed me from a heaping plate of food that seemed to appear out of nowhere. "Child needs feeding," she muttered to herself as she began shoveling gigantic spoonfuls of food into my mouth. Every once in a while she would grumble something like, "Leave it up to Rupert to be takin' in some little lost white child." I almost said I wasn't a little lost white child, but then I realized that maybe I was. When the plate was empty, I had never been so full in my life.

"Rupert's at rest now, child," she said wiping my face hard with a napkin. She licked her thumb and worked on a stubborn spot on my cheek. "Rupert's in a better place." I nodded, but wanted to tell her that what needed to be is that it needed to be summer again and Rupert needed to be with me again, walking to some church, or relaxing on the porch, or sitting at the piano banging away while laughing at me dancing and singing on the coffee table. But those words went unsaid and instead stayed in my head. She stood up from her chair, and I did too. She was sending me home. She walked me over to the basement door and stepped outside with me.

"You gotta just keep remembering, child," she said as she dusted me off and tucked my shirt in for me, "You have to keep remembering that you loved Rupert, and Rupert loved you, and now he's in a better place." Again I nodded my head, wanting to say that although that might be, I was now in a worse place being in a world where he wasn't.

"He's with Jesus in the better place," she went on. She took a hard look at me and then muttered, "Rupert, what was you thinking taking in and nursing this scrawny baby bird?" When she was satisfied that I was as straightened out as I could be, she cupped my chin in her hand and looked at me long and hard, almost seeming to be memorizing my face. She gave me one last look and then got a terribly sad face on and dabbed a tear from her eye with a floral handkerchief from the folds of her dress. She pulled me close for a quick hug that swallowed me up in her huge body. Then just as quickly she pushed me away. With tears in her eyes, Violet said, "You go back to your own people before I try keeping you for myself."

She helped me on with my backpack, then, reaching back into the pocket of her dress, she pulled out Rupert's Bible. At first, I thought she was just going to give me the photos of me and him, but instead she handed me the Bible itself with the photos inside. "He would have wanted you to have this," she said. I opened my mouth to protest, never imagining that I could accept such a precious gift, but she stopped me before I could. "I know my Rupert; he would have wanted you to have it," she said gently. Then composing herself, she ordered, "Now git." I nodded, thinking that I might start to cry if I stayed any longer. I turned and ran away. I didn't stop running until I was three blocks from the church. Then, I slowly walked the three miles back to my house.

That night I tossed and turned fitfully in my sleep. At three o'clock in the morning I awoke, soaked with sweat. I went to the window and looked out. It was raining. Blasts of thunder startled me completely awake and made my heart skip a beat. I couldn't stand the sight of the rain as it sprayed the window with drops. All I could think of was that I had left Rupert out in the rain. I had left my best friend in a hole in the ground covered in dirt, and now I had left him out in the rain.

I wondered if everyone who's buried someone feels that way at some point or another, or if grownups already realize that there's just nothing else you can do. "I'm sorry, Rupert," I cried, staring into the blackness. "I'm sorry." I knew that there was no way I was going to be able to go back to sleep. I needed closure. Rupert spoke to me, helping me to find it.

On the night table next to the bed I retrieved a tablet and pencil. I sat on the floor between the bed and window with my back up against the bed and the tablet balancing on my knees. I stared into the darkness and wrote Rupert my goodbye. I wrote, "Rupert William Holmes III home to heaven." I knew that I could not and would never let go of him completely. A part of him would always be where I was and in what I did. Even at ten I knew that much about loving and losing. I knew that when love runs that deep, then that person is always a part of you, no matter what happens. I knew that Rupert would especially be part of my music.

And for the first time, I think I really believed him. Music was always going to be in my life, and Rupert would be the life in that music. And just like he always said, "Music from the heart writes itself; all you need to do is hold the pencil." So that night I held the pencil, and, with a heart swelling with sorrow and eyes filling with tears, I watched as Rupert's song wrote itself. My teardrops fell onto the pages and arranged themselves among the musical notes and heartfelt lyrics.

The next day, before the sun came up, I snuck out of the house, holding my scrap of paper and a cross that I had made out of the root beer caps saved from the summer. I walked the three miles to Rupert's grave, watching the sun come up as I did. I climbed the hill to where he lay. I laid the cross carefully on the mound of muddy earth and talked to him for a while. Then, from the crumpled tear-stained paper, I sang to him with my whole heart. And ever so faintly I could feel him smiling and nodding and hear him singing along.

Epilogue

Rupert's song, of course, is the one that I sing at the end of every concert. I sing to my audience and to the very best friend I will ever have. With the spotlight shining in my eyes, I reach into my pocket and rub the photo strip of Rupert and me. I tell the audience that this song is for a friend of mine who in just one summer taught me to believe—to believe in God, to believe in music, and to believe in myself. I say, "This song is for all of us Believers."